Nine Lives

On the Street

Nine Lives
On the Street

As told to
Jon Saunders

Illustrated by
Emily Cornell du Houx

Polar Bear & Company
Solon, Maine

First Letter Half Edition 2015
First printing: September 2015

Polar Bear & Company™ is an imprint of the Solon Center for Research and Publishing P.O. Box 311, Solon, ME 04979, U.S.A. 207.643.2795, www.polarbearandco.org

Library of Congress Control Number: 2015948480
ISBN: 978-1-882190-39-3
Illustrations and cover design by Emily Cornell du Houx
Manufactured on acid-free paper in more than one country.

To Dianne, the Original Cat,
and to Alex and Max,
who now reside with the Great Cat.

Contents

Acknowledgments

Boo and I would like to thank all the great people who helped us with the book. Especially Renée Dunaway who put us in touch with the nice folks at the Mayor's Alliance for NYC's Animals. Evon Handras at the Alliance was particularly helpful. We'd also like to thank Dr. David Bolotin, one of Boo's earliest advocates, and Dr. Sasha Gibbons, his personal physician, as well as Boo's long-suffering groomer, Marsha Pascoe, all at Just Cats. Our special thanks to Nan de Grove and Earl Vaughn for their encouragement.

Chapter One. 925 Park Avenue.
I Make a Shocking Discovery in the Kitchen.

Call me Boo.

That's not my real name. But you probably couldn't pronounce it if I told you what it is.

Boo is the name the Old Lady gave me. You might think it has something to do with Halloween, but it doesn't. She got it from a movie she saw on TV. Something about mockingbirds.

But to tell you the truth, it doesn't matter what you call me. I won't come unless I want to.

I'm a cat.

Looking back on it all, life with the Old Lady was pretty sweet. Sure, she liked to pick me up and make me sit on her lap. I didn't like that. No cat likes to be picked up. And very few of us want to sit on somebody's lap.

The Old Lady used to brush me every single day. I didn't mind that too much unless the brush got tangled and pulled my hair. It's kind of long, you see.

The best thing about living with the Old Lady was that her memory wasn't so hot. She'd forget she'd fed me, and all I'd have to do was to meow a few times like I was starving, and she'd feed me again.

The Old Lady and I lived in an apartment in a tall building in New York City.

I knew it was tall because once in a while I'd hop up on a table and look out the window. If I pressed my head against the window, I could see cars down in the street below. They looked like toys.

Mostly, it was just me and the Old Lady. Oh, she had a couple of women who came in every day. The one who did the cleaning was called Luz. She hated me.

Luz was always grumbling about my hair being all over the furniture and how fat I was. She would never say anything to the Old Lady, of course, but she was always complaining to Rose, the one who cooked the Old Lady's meals.

Rose didn't like me very much either, but she didn't talk as much as Luz.

In spite of those two, life was good.

Then one day everything changed.

I'd been asleep on the couch most of the afternoon, and although it wasn't time for dinner, I figured I'd give it a shot. If I played my cards right maybe there'd be a second or third dinner. It had happened before.

Rose had the day off, I guess. And Luz had left by then. Anyway, neither one was around, so I knew I wouldn't have to deal with either of them. I headed for the kitchen . . . meowing my head off.

That's when I saw the Old Lady lying on the floor.

I'd never seen her on the floor before. In fact, I didn't see her in the kitchen all that often, except to give me my food. But there she was. Lying real still.

I walked over to her, and right away I could tell something wasn't quite right.

I rubbed up against her—she always liked that—but she didn't move or make a sound. And she felt different. She felt cold.

I did the rub number a few more times. But I saw it wasn't going to work. I gave her a meow or two, but I knew I was wasting my breath. She wasn't going to get up.

I figured there was no use in both of us lying on the cold floor, so I hopped up onto her bed and settled myself in.

Usually, a TV set was on someplace in the apartment, but not this time. There wasn't anything else to do, so I took a nap.

I woke up a little while later, and now I was really hungry. I prowled around the apartment, hoping that maybe the Old Lady had left some snacks out. No luck.

I glanced in the kitchen. The Old Lady was still lying there.

I looked out the window for a while.

I walked around on a table.

I sat on the sofa where the Old Lady usually sat.

I looked in the kitchen again.

Then I went back to bed.

Next thing I knew it was morning. The reason I knew was because of the sunlight coming in through the windows. That and Luz screaming her head off.

Pretty soon, old Mrs. Nussbaum from down the hall

was at our door. Luz was crying and screaming in Spanish. Mrs. Nussbaum pushed her aside and went into the kitchen.

She told Luz to shut up. Then she made a phone call. I heard her say a woman was dead.

Luz had finally quieted down by the time the police arrived. They were big humans with heavy shoes. I didn't want any part of them, so I hid under the sofa.

"She lived alone," I heard Mrs. Nussbaum say to one of the policemen. "Just her and her cat."

"Her and her cat lived pretty well, from the looks of things," the policeman said.

Mrs. Nussbaum told them she didn't think the Old Lady had any relatives and only a few friends.

"She had a banker—a personal banker—who came by sometimes and, once in awhile, her lawyer. I don't know their names, but if you want I could look around and . . ."

"That won't be necessary," the policeman said. "We got somebody at headquarters who does that. She'll come by later."

"What about her cat?" Mrs. Nussbaum asked. I was kind of interested in that myself.

"I didn't see a cat," the policeman said.

"You couldn't miss him. He's the fattest cat you ever saw. Long black hair."

"Hey, any of you guys seen a cat?" the policeman yelled.

None of them had. It was hard to have a lot of confidence in cops who couldn't find a cat in a living room.

"Well, if he's here, Animal Control will take him in until somebody claims him. If nobody does, they'll put him up for adoption."

"Nobody will want him," Luz sniffed. "He's fat and lazy and he sheds all over the place. Besides, black cats like him are bad luck. Just look at the Old . . . I mean the Señora."

"Good grief!" said Mrs. Nussbaum. "She was overweight—never took any exercise—and was eighty if she was a day. Luck didn't have anything to do with it."

"I'm just saying . . ." Luz said.

"What happens if he's not adopted?" Mrs. Nussbaum asked the policeman.

"Well . . ." the policeman just kind of trailed off.

I didn't like where this was going.

Just then some humans in white clothes came with a table on wheels. I could see them lift the Old Lady onto it. It wasn't easy; she was kind of heavy. We had that in common.

When they opened the door, I made a split-second decision. Which was to run for it as fast as I could. I may be a little overweight, or at least I was back then, but I could move when I had to.

I was through the door and down the hall before anybody knew what was happening. I wasn't going to let Animal Control take control of me.

As luck would have it, the door to the stairway was open. A good thing, since I would have never been able to push the buttons in the elevator. I headed down the stairs. It took a long time to get to the first floor, and I was out of breath by the time I did.

The doorman and the super were standing by the front door looking anxious. I guess they wanted to get the Old Lady out of there as fast as possible. Having a dead tenant was probably bad for business.

The doorman had to open the door for some female carrying packages. I got my second wind and shot past them out into the street.

I hadn't ever actually been on a street before. Not without being inside a cat carrier, that is. There were people everywhere. And cars and taxis in the streets. I figured I was better off staying close to the buildings.

I knew from the Old Lady that we lived on a street called Park Avenue. And that was about all I knew about the world outside our apartment.

I was about to find out more than I ever wanted to know.

Chapter Two. Park Avenue and 81st Street.
I Am Chased by Dogs and Doormen and Humiliated by an Alley Cat.

I was really hungry by now—hungrier than I could ever remember being. I had to find something to eat.

I also had another problem. This morning had been so crazy I didn't get a chance to use my litter box. And now I needed to. Bad.

I walked along Park for a while, staying close to the buildings, when I saw the answer to at least one of my problems. There, next to a doorway, was a big pot filled with sand. An outdoor litter box! Only in New York, as the Old Lady would say.

It was a little high off the sidewalk, so I had to climb up a couple of steps to get over to it.

"Who would put cigarette butts in a cat's litter box?" I wondered as I did my morning business.

Just then a little human walking along with her mother spied me. "Mommy! Look at the kitty pooing!"

Up until then, the building's doorman had been busy talking to another human, but when he heard the kid, he saw me and started yelling. He couldn't quite figure out what to do about me and by the time he did, I was finished. I jumped down and ran off. I didn't bury, but it wasn't my fault. I was in a hurry. I was afraid the human would get all his fellow doormen together and start chasing me, so I ran for it.

Right into a pack of dogs.

A small female human had six of them on leashes. But when they saw me, they broke away from her and started after me. There I was, with a mob of crazed doormen behind me and a pack of wild dogs in front of me. Only one place to run. The street. Park Avenue.

I could hear brakes screeching, horns blowing, and humans yelling as I ran to a little concrete island in the middle of the street. I looked back to the sidewalk. I couldn't believe I had made it. Cars were everywhere. How was I ever going to get across?

"Look, Tommy. That poor cat can't cross the street. He must be terrified."

It was a pretty, young female human waiting to cross the street. She was with a big, goofy looking human male.

"Go help him," the female human told the male.

"Here you go, kitty," the male human said as he picked me up.

"Hey! Stop squirming. I'm not going to hurt you."

Of course, I was squirming. The big lummox was taking me right back to the place I'd just run away from.

He put me down on the sidewalk. I looked around for the doormen and the dogs. I didn't see either. But I decided I'd had enough of Park Avenue for a while. I turned down a side street.

This street was quieter with fewer taxis. I was walking along . . . keeping my eyes open . . . when I passed an alley. Almost immediately, I smelled food. I turned into the alley and headed straight for where the smell was coming from—a big garbage can.

Now, I'd never eaten out of a garbage can in my life. But the food smelled OK. And I was starving.

I figured one good jump and I'd be on top of the can. I was just about to leap when something popped out of it.

It was another cat.

It took me a second or two to realize that, though. This cat looked like no cat I'd ever seen. Some of his hair was missing . . . so was part of his ear. And his left eye was almost closed.

"Get your own, Fats! This here's mine."

"Sorry, I didn't know it was yours," I managed to say. "I'm just looking for some food."

"Yeah, well, look someplace else. This is my can and my alley. So beat it."

If I hadn't been so hungry, I would have done just that.

"Could you tell me where I might find some food?" I asked the alley cat.

"What do I look like, *Zagat's?* Anyway, you don't look like you've missed too many meals."

"Well, I didn't until yesterday. You see, my human died, and I don't have anyone to feed me."

"Hey, things are tough all over. Now scram, so I can finish my dinner."

"Would there be enough to share?"

"Share? Are you for real?" With that the cat jumped down from his can. His fur seemed to be wearing out, like an old sweater. He put his face right in mine. His breath smelled awful.

"Don't you know cats are territorial? I marked this alley good and proper. Now, for the last time, get outta here or I'll rip all that nice long hair right off your back."

"OK," I said and started to slink away.

"Are you gone take that from that cat?"

I turned. It was a female cat. I couldn't tell if she was my age or a lot older. She looked a little better than the alley cat but not much.

"You twice as big as he is. You gone let him push you around like that?"

"I guess so. I don't know what else to do."

"Don't you know how to fight?"

"No, not really. I mean I never had to."

Truth was, I really didn't know much about other cats. Sure, I'd exchanged a few meows at the vet's, but that was about it. It's hard to have a conversation when you're locked in a portable cage.

"Honey, you gone have a tough time if you don't learn pretty quick. What you doin' out here anyway? Your human throw you out?"

I told her about the Old Lady being dead.

"Yeah, they do that sometimes. Die on you."

I asked her where I might find something to eat—that I didn't have to fight for.

"You might try the subway. Plenty of rats down there—but you got to watch out for the trains."

"I've never eaten a rat before. Not sure I know how."

"What about birds? You ever catch a bird?"

I confessed I hadn't.

"Honey, you best find yourself a human to take care of you . . . You not gone make it on the streets."

I nodded. I was afraid she was right.

"And you better do it soon—while you still got your looks. Before you hair get all matted and dirty. Won't no human want you then."

"But I don't know any humans. Except Luz and Rose and Mrs. Nussbaum, and they don't like me very much."

"Plenty of other humans around. Just do that cute kitty number. They suckers for that."

"I was kind of hoping I could come home with you for a little while . . ." I said.

"Home!" the cat said sadly. "Honey, this is my home."

I didn't know what to say. The cat started walking away.

"Try over on Lex," she called over her shoulder. "Some delis and restaurants there."

She was gone before I could ask her which way this "Lex" might be.

Chapter Three. Lexington Avenue.
I Am Robbed and Make a Dangerous Enemy.

As it turned out, Lex was a street even busier and more dangerous than Park Avenue. The sidewalks were narrower, and all the humans seemed to be in a hurry.

Nobody paid any attention to me. I had to stay close to the buildings to keep from getting stepped on. There wasn't any food on that block, and I really didn't want to cross the street. I was standing there on the curb, trying to decide what to do, when somebody decided for me.

"Gotcha!" the human said as he grabbed me. Like I told you, I don't like to be picked up, but it happened so fast I couldn't do anything about it.

"Hey, look! I got me a pussy cat," the human was saying. There were three of them. Young humans, kind of skinny and nervous-looking, with sketchy hair on their faces.

"Whattaya gonna do with a cat?" one of them asked.

I was squirming in the human's arms, but he was holding me really tight.

I could hardly breathe.

"This big fat cat is gonna buy us some stuff, man. Good stuff."

"Whattaya mean?" one of the other humans asked.

"Look at this cat. I'm guessing Park Avenue, and I'm guessing two words. Re . . . ward."

"You think somebody gonna pay for a cat?"

The human was fiddling with my collar all this time—trying to turn it so he could read what was written on it.

"What did I tell you?" he said. "Apartment 16A, 925 Park Avenue. Bingo!"

"Are you nuts?" It was the biggest human of the three, not that any of them were all that big. Up to that point, he hadn't said anything. When he did, the others seemed to pay attention to him. I guess he was their leader.

"First place, we'll look like idiots carrying a cat around. Second place, nobody's gonna believe we didn't steal it. We'll get busted for sure. I got a better idea. Gimme the cat."

The human holding me handed me to the leader-human.

"See, we just take his collar, right? Looks like it silver or somethin'. Maybe Pops give us a few bucks for it."

The human held me up so he could get a good look at my collar. I had a bad feeling about this.

"Yeah, gotta be worth plenty," one of the other humans said.

"Good idea, man," the other one said.

The other humans worked on my collar while their leader held me. It seemed to take forever, but eventually they figured out how to get it off.

"OK, let's go see Pops and find out what this thing's worth."

"What about the cat?" one of other human asked?

"Let's see if he can land on his feet."

With that, the human lifted me up over his head like he was going to smash me on the sidewalk. I panicked and gave him a good swipe across the face. I didn't really mean to. It was just reflex.

"My eye!" he screamed. "This cat's put my eye out! I'm blind!"

He dropped me, and I ran as fast as I could. Then I hid in an alley and waited for a long time. I waited until I was sure those humans were nowhere around. Then I waited some more.

Finally, I came out. They were gone.

But so was my collar.

To be honest, I never cared much for that collar. I didn't really need one, being inside all the time. But the Old Lady wanted me to have one, so I did.

She got it from a place called Tiffany's.

It was the way those humans had taken my collar that really bothered me. It made me feel like I'd felt in the alley with that awful cat. I was feeling pretty low and really hungry by that time. I had no collar and no home. I didn't think things could get much worse.

Then, they did.

It started to rain.

I don't know about you, but I hate to get wet. It makes my fur clump up something awful. I found a doorway that had a little awning over it. The place didn't look very busy, so I figured I'd wait there for the rain to stop.

I was just waiting there . . . not bothering anybody . . . when a female came out of the place and started yelling at me. I didn't want to get wet, so I tried to look as adorable as possible.

She disappeared inside for a minute and came back with a broom. So much for adorable. I moved on. Out into the rain.

Pretty soon, I was soaked. My hair takes in water like a sponge. I could see my reflection in some of the lower store windows. I looked terrible.

Eventually it stopped raining, and I found a grate on the sidewalk with hot air coming out of it. I sat on it until I was a little less wet. Then I went looking for something to eat.

I decided to head back toward Park Avenue, where people seemed a little less likely to try and kidnap me. I wandered down Park hoping to find a careless hot dog vendor who might drop my next meal. No such luck. I guess not many people eat hot dogs on Park Avenue.

Eventually, I came to a big, old building that I recognized as a church. I'd only seen one real church. The Old Lady took me to one downtown for something called a "blessing of animals." She complained about that church being too "low" for her, although it looked tall enough to me. Anyway, we never went back. All of us animals found the whole blessing thing pretty embarrassing, so it was just as well.

Maybe this was the same church the Old Lady went to. She went in the mornings, but they seemed to be open for business now. At least, the door was open.

It was dark inside the church, and there didn't seem to be anybody around. But there was a big table way down the aisle at the front of the church. And where there's a table, there's bound to be food.

Even though the place seemed empty, I figured I had to be careful. So I slowly made my way toward the table. There was a kind of rail between the table and the seats, but the gate was open.

The table was covered with a green-and-white cloth. It was pretty high off the floor. I figured it was within my range, so I jumped.

Bummer! There wasn't any food on the table. Just some silver dishes. Just then a couple of humans came in from a side door. The old human was giving the young one a hard time about something.

"I don't care if you had to go. You just can't leave the—"

Then he saw me and started yelling.

"Look! A . . . cat! Get him off the altar!"

Time to go.

The human had startled me, so naturally my claws were out. Which was unfortunate because they got tangled in the tablecloth when I jumped down.

There was a huge crash, and all the silver stuff fell on the floor. Some white crackers had fallen out of one of the containers, but I was in too much of a hurry to grab one.

Now a couple of other humans were coming after me. I darted in and out between rows of seats until I made it through the door and onto the street Those humans never had a prayer of catching me. Not with those long dresses they were wearing.

But I was still starving. I hadn't eaten all day, and I was beginning to think I wouldn't last until tomorrow.

I was about to give up on Park and head east again, when I saw it. It was some kind of little cart, and it had a little human in it. The little human looked too big to be in a cart like that. But I was more interested in what he had in his hands. Dinner!

I eased my way to the cart and stood up on my back legs. The little human looked glad to see me. I guess he was bored. The female human who was supposed to be watching him was busy chattering away on her cell phone.

He pointed the top of his bottle in my direction, and

I took that as an invitation. It didn't take long to get the hang of it, and I started helping myself to the milk. It was delicious.

Unfortunately, the female human happened to look down and started screaming that I was trying to take the baby's breath. Of course, I wouldn't do such a thing, even if I knew how. What would I do with a baby's breath, anyway? I was only interested in the milk.

I was well around the corner by the time the policeman got there.

The milk helped a little, but I was still hungry. I was used to eating maybe a dozen times a day. The Old Lady made sure there was always dry food in my bowl. And a can every morning and every night. Sometimes more if she forgot.

It was getting dark. If I were home, I'd be chowing down on a bowl full of Little Friskies right about now. Or maybe not. The Old Lady wouldn't be there to feed me. And I was pretty sure Luz or Rose wouldn't.

I finally found half a slice of pizza someone had thrown in a trash can. There was a cigarette butt in the middle, but I ate around it. I figured that was it for dinner and went looking for a place to sleep.

I walked down the street, keeping my eyes open for a safe one. Finally, I settled for a spot under the steps of a house. I figured I'd doze a bit and then go looking for something else to eat. I was still hungry.

Chapter Four. Park and 79th.
I Break into the Movies.

Even though I was dead tired, I didn't sleep all that well. I'd doze for a couple of minutes and then wake up with a start. Being hungry didn't help much, either.

Finally, it started to get a little less dark. A new day was dawning, as they say. A new day on the street. This street thing was getting old already, and I'd only been doing it for one day. Gradually, I realized that there was another sunrise—only this one was coming from the wrong direction. West. I had to check this out.

I crawled out from under the steps and looked around. I didn't see any humans but, just to be safe, I sidled along next to the buildings as much as possible. There were a lot of big trucks parked along the street where it runs into Park Avenue and a lot of humans, too. Big guys, for the most part, just standing around and drinking coffee out of Styrofoam cups. They didn't pay me any attention.

It still wasn't daylight by the time I got to Park, but you would have never known it. There were huge lights that lit up the street like it was the middle of the day or at least morning. But what got my attention was something I couldn't see but I sure could smell.

Food.

The problem was how to get to it. The side street was beginning to fill up with those big humans, and I was a little concerned about getting stepped on or run over by the equipment they were wheeling around. I decided to wait over in the shadows until things quieted down.

Most of the action was taking place on that narrow strip of concrete that divides Park Avenue—like the place I'd run to when the dogs and doormen were chasing me. That's where the lights were set up and the humans were going with the equipment.

What interested me was on my side of Park. About halfway down the block was a big table loaded down with what smelled like breakfast. Eggs, bacon, ham, bagels and lox—you name it, it was in the air, and it was coming from that table.

I carefully made my way along the buildings. The table was surrounded by big humans. A couple of female humans were busy shoveling food into plates and passing them over to the humans. I hid in the shadows and bided my time.

I was worried that those big humans would eat all the food, and there'd be none left for me. But after what seemed hours, the crowd thinned out.

Then I heard somebody say over some kind of loudspeaker, "Quiet everybody . . . this is a take," and everybody got real still. Everybody turned toward the middle of the street, and I figured it was about time to make my move.

Another voice shouted, "Action!" and I took that as

my cue. I hopped up on the table and made straight for the bacon—I love the stuff. I'd planned to grab a few pieces then jump down. But when I saw all that food, I just couldn't help myself. I started chowing down on everything in sight.

I'd thought everybody's attention was on what was happening in the middle of the street. I was wrong. One of the females who'd been behind the table turned and spotted me and screamed.

When she did, one of the big humans made a grab for me, but I was well on my way across Park. I might have mentioned that I can move pretty fast when I have to, and this was one of those times when I had to.

Nobody on the divider had noticed what had happened at the food table, so I figured I was safe for a while. I was kind of curious as to what was going on, so I made my way to the edge, so I could see the other side of the street.

What I saw was the most beautiful female human I had ever seen. She had stepped off the sidewalk and was trying to hail a taxi. A yellow cab rolled up and stopped. Just as she opened the door to get in, a male human yelled "Susan! Wait!" and ran up to her.

Then a voice yelled, "Cut!" and they stopped right where they were.

That's when I realized what was going on. They were making a television show. I had seen something like this on the Old Lady's TV set, but I hadn't paid it any attention.

Another human had come over from the divider and was talking to the two humans. Pretty soon he walked back. I couldn't see where he went, but another voice said,

"OK, places. This is a take."

I watched them do that maybe half a dozen times. Always the same thing. The female never got in the taxi. The human would yell "Cut!" and then they'd do the whole thing over.

I was getting a little bored by now and was beginning to wonder if I dared to try for the food again. I moved out from between the two boxes that had hidden me from the humans and turned to check out the other side of the street.

As luck would have it, the human who had chased me before spotted me. I didn't have a choice. I had to run across the street toward the beautiful female and her taxi.

I heard the human yell, "CUT!" again, but by that time I was on the other side. I stopped and looked up. I was right at the feet of the beautiful female. I was so mesmerized that I didn't see the big male human who scooped me up.

"Oh, don't hurt him!" the beautiful female human squealed. "Here, give him to me!"

She took me from the big human and held me in her arms. "What a gorgeous kitty you are! Where did you come from?"

I don't think she expected me to answer. It's just the kind of thing some people say to cats if they like them.

The human who'd been yelling "cut" had run over by this time, and she held me up so he could see.

"Look at the gorgeous kitty, Marty. Isn't he the sweetest thing you ever saw?"

"Yeah, he's sweet, Simone. But I'd just as soon not see him in my shot."

"Well, he didn't know. He's just a lost, little kitty cat."

"He probably lives around here. Why don't we let him find his way home, so we can finish shooting this scene?"

"Oh no, Marty. See, he doesn't have a collar. He's all

alone out here."

"Tell you what," the male human said. "Let's take him back to your Winnebago, where he'll be safe and we can finish our scene."

"Well, all right. But make sure nobody hurts him. And give him something to eat!"

The male human muttered something to himself I couldn't quite make out and walked back across the street holding me. He handed me to a burly male human and said, "Take care of the cat!"

"You mean . . . take care . . . of him?" the human said.

"No . . . no . . . don't hurt him. Just take him back to her Winnebago and get somebody to watch him."

The big human walked over to two young female humans. "Marty wants you should take care of Simone's cat."

"Her cat? Now we've got to look after her cat?" one of the females sniffed.

"If you ever want to work on one of his pictures again, you do. Just take him back to one of the Winnebagos, and feed him and brush him or something."

"Sure, we've got this," the other female said. "C'mon, Syl. We're not PAs anymore. We got promoted to cat groomers."

I could tell they didn't know much about cats from the way they were carrying me. Finally, we got to the "Winnebago," which turned out to be like a small house on a truck. But the females turned out to be nice enough. One got me some lox and other stuff from the food table, and they took turns brushing me.

They got bored with that after a while and left me alone while they talked and talked. I learned from their chatter that they weren't making a TV show at all; it was something called a "feature," which I found out was a movie. I had never seen a real movie, except on television. And now I was in one. Or one scene of one, anyway.

I was sort of expecting the beautiful female to stop in and check on me. But I told myself she was busy. She'd come by later and take me home with her. I fell asleep thinking how nice it would be to have that pretty female for my human.

Next thing I knew, a human was banging on the Winnebago's door. But it wasn't the pretty one. It was a big male.

"Let's go ladies. We've wrapped."

"What about her cat? Simone's cat, I mean," one of the females asked.

"She's halfway to London by now. Raoul showed up, and she split right after the taxi scene."

"What about her cat?" the female asked again.

"She's forgot all about that cat. Just let him go."

One of the females said she wanted to keep me but was afraid her boyfriend wouldn't want a cat. The other said she thought a cat might get in the way of her "career."

They kept telling each other I'd find my way back to my home. But I think they said that just to make themselves feel better. They opened the door and put me on the sidewalk.

One minute I was some beautiful female's "gorgeous little kitty" and the next I was back on the street again. It was as if the whole thing had never happened.

I guess that's show business.

Chapter Five. Lex and 73rd.
I Am Set Upon by Gangster Cats.

I went back to my place under the steps and decided to catch a few Zs before going out to look for dinner. Even though I'd slept most of the day, I went to sleep right away. When I woke up, it was pitch dark.

There were fewer people on the sidewalks and not so many cars in the street. I figured it was safe enough to try to cross one.

I walked along until I found a bunch of black plastic bags piled on the sidewalk in front of what I guessed was a place where humans go to eat. "A restaurant," I think they're called.

The bags were just lying there on the sidewalk, and it was easy to get to what was inside. Which I did right away.

I couldn't believe my eyes. There was all sorts of food in there. Fish . . . meat . . . and stuff I couldn't identify. But it looked delicious.

This was going to be OK, I thought. I could live on the streets and take care of myself. I didn't need beautiful female humans. I didn't need any humans! I could do this!

I was just about to chow down on part of a thick, juicy steak, when I heard a voice.

"Hey fleabag! Whattaya think you're doin'?"

I looked around to see four of the meanest-looking cats I could imagine.

"This is our territory," one of the cats said. "And we didn't send out no dinner invitations. Now, get away from our chow."

I didn't see that I had a choice. I was surrounded on all sides.

"Hey Skip, maybe he's from that Uptown crew," one of the cats was saying.

"I'm not from any . . . *crew* . . . whatever that is. I'm just trying to get a bite to eat," I said.

"Hah! We'll give you a bite all right. We don't like tourists on our turf."

"I didn't know it was your . . . turf. But . . . hey . . . it's late. I've got to be going—"

"Not so fast, fatso. You think you can just eat and run?"

"Well, actually I didn't really eat anything."

"Oh a wise guy, eh? Spike show this chowhound what we do to wise guys."

Before I knew what was happening, the cat called Spike gave me a swipe across the face. Claws out. I was stunned. I'd never had a paw laid on me before.

"C'mon, you can do better than that. Guys—help him out."

That's when the cats jumped me. Three of them—all at once.

I had never been in a fight in my life, and I'm not sure this counted as one, since I wasn't doing much of the fighting. We were rolling around on that dirty sidewalk with cats clawing and biting me.

Well, not exactly. I had so much fur at that time, most of the bites and claws didn't make it to my skin. But, still, I was losing a lot of fur, and I was worried about what I might lose next.

"Wait!" I shouted. "There's something I've got to tell you."

"Yeah! Your last words," the head cat said.

"No . . . wait . . . I know where there's food—better than this . . ."

It's hard to carry on a conversation with three cats on top of you, but I knew I had to try if I was going to get off that sidewalk alive.

"OK, let him up guys. Let's hear all about this 'great' food," the head cat said.

I was out of breath and could barely talk. But I was thinking as fast as I could.

"I found a place with all kinds of great food, and it's easy to get into. I'll show you where it is."

"He's lying, Skip. We know all the places around here."

"It's not around here. It's further south." I was lying, of course. Anything to distract those cats long enough to make a break for it.

"Close but no cigar," the head cat said. He turned to the other cats. "OK, guys, finish him off."

"Wait . . . this place . . . it's a place where you can get a nice, juicy mouse. All the mice you want, in fact."

"And where might this place be?"

I remembered what the female cat had told me. I hoped she was right. "The subway," I said.

"The subway? There's no mice in the subway. Nothing but rats."

"Well, rats then. Nice, big, juicy rats . . . I'll bring you one . . . no . . . all you want."

"You telling me you're gonna go down in the subway and bring me a rat?"

"Sure. I had one last night. Kind of gamey but really delicious."

The big cat thought for a moment. He had a smile on his face.

"OK, wise guy. You bring us each one of those subway rats and we let you go."

"Great!" I said. "I'll be right back."

"Not so fast, hotshot. Why don't we wait a little while? Rats won't come out until late . . . when all the humans are gone."

He turned to the three cats who'd jumped me. "Keep an eye on our friend here. Make sure he don't get no bright ideas about leaving us."

So we settled down to an uneasy wait. The other cats growled at me from time to time. I pretended to sleep, but I was really wide awake and worried.

Maybe a couple of hours had gone by. It seemed a lot longer. Finally, the one the one they called the Skipper came over to us.

"Showtime, fat boy. Go get me a rat."

He nodded to the three cats and said, "Two of youse go along and keep our friend company on his little shopping trip."

He said something else to the cats, but I couldn't make out what. Then he shot me a funny look, and the three of us headed for the subway.

Chapter Six. 77th Street Station.
I Face Certain Death Beneath the #4 Train.

If you'd been on Lexington Avenue at that particular spot that night, you'd have seen a pretty unusual sight: three cats walking along the sidewalk, all bunched up together.

You might have thought we were good friends, hanging out. But you'd have been wrong.

My companions weren't saying anything, and neither was I. Finally, one of them turned his head and spoke in my general direction.

"I gotta tell ya . . . youse sure don't look it."

"What do you mean?"

"I mean even we don't go in the subways."

"Why not?" I asked.

"There's things down there . . . things that make noise."

"Those are called *trains*," I said. "Humans use then to get from one place to another.

"Maybe so. All I know the subway is no place for cats."

"Hey! Shut up!" the other cat snorted. "The Skip don't want us talking to him."

We padded on in silence for a little while. I tried to talk to the cat who'd spoken to me.

"Why do you call your leader 'Skip'?"

"That's what you call the head of a crew."

"You mean like on *The Sopranos*?"

"What's a Soprano?"

"Hey! I told you to shut up," the other cat growled. "Both of youse—"

The only thing I knew about subways is from what I'd seen on TV. I'd never even been close to one. The Old Lady wasn't exactly the subway type, if you know what I mean. She had a great big car and a driver named Burke. He took her wherever she wanted to go. That's how she would take me to the vet's.

I had no idea where a subway might be, but I pretended to know where I was going. I could sense that my companions were losing patience. But then I saw it. A sign I recognized as marking an entrance to the subway.

Tell me TV isn't educational.

The entrance was nothing fancy. In fact, it was pretty grim. Just a few steps leading down to a big, dirty room. There was a booth along the side of the wall about halfway down the room, but there was no one in it.

There was a gate of sorts at the end of the room, but it was meant to keep out humans, not cats. We slipped through it onto a platform.

What TV hadn't prepared me for was the smell. It was awful! The other cats didn't seem to notice, but it was making me sick.

"Well, fats, we're here. Start finding those rats you were mouthing off about," one of my guards said.

Both of the cats hung back near the gate. I could see

another gate at the other end of the platform. But it was a long way from where I was.

I went sniffing around on the platform trying hard not to breathe and pretending to look for rats at the same time. I did that for a while, carefully working my way toward the edge of the platform while the other cats watched from a distance.

I looked down on the tracks. There were two shiny rails with some wooden planks between them. Here and there were pools of greenish water. Across on the other side was another set of tracks.

When I looked up the tracks, I could see was some humans in orange jackets, but they were a long way off. They were workmen, I guessed, doing something with the tracks. I wasn't going to get any help from them.

Then I heard the sound I'd been waiting for. The tracks began to rattle, and to the far left I could see a bright light heading my way.

"Freedom," I thought.

I knew I had to make my move fast. So the minute the train pulled along next to the platform, I made it. I bolted toward that train as fast as I could go.

In my mind, I could see the train door opening and me running inside with the thug cats left waiting on the platform. Maybe I'd jump up on one of the seats and look at them through the window. Or maybe I'd just lay low for a while and go wherever the train took me.

But none of that happened. The train didn't stop. It just blew its whistle and went on past me . . .

I knew they were there without turning around.

"Think you're pretty smart, huh?" one of them was

saying. "Gonna try to get away from us. Well, the Skip had you pegged, all right. He told us you'd try something cute."

"No . . . no . . . you've got it all wrong. I thought I saw a rat. Look! There he is over there!"

With that, I started toward the gate. The other cats were right on top of me before I could take one step.

We were rolling around on that filthy subway platform. They were trying to bite and claw me; I was just trying to get away. We had no idea how close to the edge of the platform we were. That is, until we realized all at once that there was nothing under us.

I tried to twist my body so I'd land on my feet. Unfortunately, the other cats were trying to do the same thing. Our twists canceled each other out, and we hit hard. For a moment we just lay there on the tracks. A tangled mass of panting cats.

One of the cats pulled free and started to say something, then stopped. His eyes got really wide.

The tracks were beginning to shake and rattle. Another train was coming.

Without so much as a word, both cats tensed themselves up and jumped for the platform. They made it easily and promptly disappeared from view.

I knew I had to try to jump, too, but that platform looked awfully high. I'd never jumped that high in my life. Besides, even if I did manage to reach the platform, those cats might be up there waiting for me.

There was another set of tracks, but they were all the way over on the other side of the tunnel. Maybe I could get to them and I'd be safe.

I kept trying to remember what I'd heard about subway tracks. Something about a "third rail" and that it could kill you if you touched it.

Third rail or not, I knew this was my only chance. So I ran for the other side as fast as I could.

I was panting and shaking all over when I got there, but for a moment I was safe. That is, until I realized it wasn't me shaking. It was the tracks I was on. Two trains coming in different directions with me on the tracks! What are the odds of that?

I looked about for some space I could wedge myself into, but to tell the truth I was beginning to panic. I didn't see any spaces like that, and the trains were getting closer. There was only one thing to do. The platform was high and probably well beyond my range, but I knew I had to try.

I squeezed my muscles together on that rattling track. I took a deep breath. And then I jumped—jumped with every muscle in my body—with everything I had in me.

And missed.

I must have hit my head or something when I came back down because all of a sudden I felt dizzy and couldn't move. And with a subway train bearing down on me.

This was it. Me and the Old Lady in the same week.

Chapter Seven. Myrtle Avenue.
I Visit Brooklyn and Temporarily Become "Twinkie."

"Gotcha," the voice said.

I could feel strong arms around me lifting me up off the tracks. The train roared by inches from my face.

"You're OK now," the voice said. It was a big voice but a kindly one. Whoever owned the voice was holding me in his arms. I could tell he never held a cat before. But I didn't mind. He'd saved my life.

"Looks like you got yourself a kitty cat," I heard another voice say.

"Yeah, it's a good thing we were here, or this would be one flat cat."

I could look around a little now. Those humans who'd been working on the track must have come up to the platform area. One of them had grabbed me off the tracks.

"What you gonna do with him?" one of the humans asked.

"I dunno . . . put him back up on the platform and let him go, I guess."

"Why don't you take him home to your little girl? He don't have no collar or nothin'. Don't belong to nobody."

"Well, I guess I could. She got a birthday comin' up, and this could be her present."

"Yeah, you get off cheap that way," the other human said.

"How am I supposed to get this cat home? I can't hold him all the way to Brooklyn."

"Here, I'll punch some holes in this drink box—"

The other human took some kind of tool and punched holes in a white Styrofoam chest. When he'd finished, the one holding me eased me into it. It was a tight fit.

"There, cat" the human said. "Let's go home."

The holes were big enough so I could get air but not so big that I could see out of them. I could feel movement, and it seemed we were getting on a cart of some kind. In a couple of minutes, it began to move—fast.

We zipped along for what seemed like a long time. Finally, we got off the moving cart. The humans all said goodnight to each other. Then the human carrying me walked for a few steps, and then I could tell he was sitting down.

"Cat, if you promise not to jump out of this box, I'll slide the lid back a little."

With that he opened the lid a couple of inches, and I poked my nose into the opening. He slid the lid back a little more so I could get my head out and look around.

I was in a subway car.

"Better to be in one than under one," I thought. I turned to look at my rescuer. He was a big human, and he was wearing some kind of orange vest over a tan shirt. The white helmet he'd been wearing was on the seat next to him. The big human had a friendly smile and brown skin. I meowed a greeting.

"You'll be all right, cat," he said. "Lisa's goin' to love you."

I'd been so scared that, for the first time in my life, I had completely forgotten about food. But now that I was safe, that old empty feeling in my stomach was coming back. I meowed again.

"I bet you hungry," he said. "I got nothin' but this, though. I don't know if cats eat Twinkies."

He had taken a little yellow cake out of his shirt pocket. He broke it in half and held it close to my mouth. It was gone in an instant. I never had a Twinkie before—but this one was delicious.

"You *are* hungry. Might as well have the rest."

I finished the human's Twinkie and hoped there'd be more. But he had told the truth. I was still hungry.

The rest of the way, the human talked to me about his little girl and how excited she was going to be when she saw me. I tried to listen, but I was exhausted from my adventures in the subway. I fell asleep in that container on a train to Brooklyn.

I woke up as the Big Human was carrying me up the stairs from a subway station. It was less dark than it had been when the cats and I went into that other station. I couldn't see much from the box, but I guessed the sun would be up soon.

He carried me along for a couple of blocks, then up some steps and we were inside. He set my box down while he fumbled with some keys.

"Joe . . . what in the world?" I heard a female say. She sounded a little annoyed.

"This here's a little something I got for Lisa. For her birthday."

He opened the box, and I looked around. The woman looked at me like she'd never seen a cat before.

"A cat? You bought her a cat?"

"No, I found him. On the tracks at the 77th Street station. He was about to get run over."

"Joe, you know that's somebody's cat. He looks like one of those pedigreed cats you see on TV. We can't keep him."

"How you figure that?" he said. "He's got no collar . . . no tag. Besides I saved his life . . . guess that gives me some kinda rights."

"Well, how do we know he doesn't have some kind of disease being down there in that subway? Or fleas?"

Fleas! I was insulted. Sure, I'd heard of fleas, but I'd never experienced one.

I wasn't even sure what a flea was. All I knew was I didn't have any. Unless I'd picked one up from those gangster cats.

"I'll get him one of those flea collars tomorrow. He can stay here in the kitchen tonight."

Just then the door opened. A little human girl was standing there rubbing her eyes as if she just woke up. She stood there for a second or two. Then she saw me. Next thing I knew, the little girl had picked me up and was squeezing me tight.

"Oh Daddy . . . a kitty!"

"Well, we'll have to see . . ." the female was saying. But the little girl wasn't listening.

"What's his name?" she asked.

"You might call him Lucky," the man said. "But I guess you get to name him.

All I know about him is he was on the tracks, and he likes Twinkies."

"That's what I'll call him. Twinkie."

"Now, he needs to stay in the kitchen tonight. Lisa . . ." the female said. But the little girl was already on the way back to her room with me in her arms.

That's when she started sneezing.

Now, I don't know about all cats, but those I've talked with and I agree on one thing. When it comes to humans, we tend to like the young, pretty female kind. They smell nice, and they're almost always gentle.

The Old Lady wasn't young or pretty by any means. But she was kind and gave me plenty to eat. In my book, that's almost as good.

Anyhow, I knew I'd get along fine with the Little Girl. She was very young and very pretty. And she seemed to like me a lot.

If she would only stop sneezing. It was keeping us both awake.

I guess we managed to get some sleep, because next thing I knew it was morning. The Big Human had gone someplace, and the Little Girl's mother was cooking breakfast.

It smelled delicious.

But it turned out, the breakfast wasn't for me. I just got a bowl of milk by the refrigerator. It was a good start, but I was still hungry.

The Little Girl's mother kept asking her how she felt. She seemed to think she'd caught a cold from running around barefoot in the middle of the night. Or not getting enough sleep. Or something.

Pretty soon, the Big Human came back with a couple of shopping bags. He'd bought a flea collar for me and a litter box. I wasn't crazy about wearing a flea collar, but I was glad to see that litter box. I'd been eyeing a big flower pot in the living room just in case, and I was fairly certain using it wouldn't endear me to the female human.

But even better than the litter box were the cans of food the Big Human had bought me. I could tell they weren't the brands the Old Lady bought, but they'd do.

I'd just polished off a can when another human arrived. She was an old human—maybe as old as the Old Lady—but not nearly as fat.

I could tell I was going to have trouble with this one.

"A cat!" she shrieked. "How am I supposed to look after this baby and a cat?"

"I don't think he's going to need much looking after," the Little Girl's mother said.

"Well, he better stay out of my way. I don't like cats."

"No kidding," I thought.

The Little Girl and I did a pretty good job of staying out of the Old Human's way. We spent most of the day in her room. I was a guest at a make-believe tea party; then she tried some of her doll's clothes on me.

Ordinarily, I wouldn't have put up with any of that, but for some reason I felt like going along with it. Maybe I figured I owed her. After all, her father had saved my life.

She told me the Old Human was her grandmother and that she looked after her while her mother was at work. Her father slept most of the day because he worked nights in the subway.

The Old Human didn't bother us much. The only time we saw her was when she gave the Little Girl lunch. She spent most of the day dozing in front of the television set. I had seen the Old Lady do that plenty of times.

I guess it's something old humans do.

Chapter Eight. Grand Central Station.
I Become a Disciple and a Cat Servant.

That's pretty much how it went for the next few weeks. I had a roof over my head, a safe place to sleep, and three square meals a day. (OK, more than three—the Little Girl was always sneaking me extra food.)

Life was good.

Only problem was the Little Girl was always sneezing and had to blow her nose a lot.

One day her mother asked a neighbor to come in and take a look at the Little Girl. The neighbor wore a white uniform. She was what they call a nurse.

"I'd say it's some sort of allergy," the nurse said. "When did she start?"

"Three weeks ago," her mother said. "The night Joe brought home that cat."

"Well, there you go," the nurse said. "She's probably

allergic to the thing."

"I hope not. Lisa loves that cat."

"Well, you might not have to get rid of it. You know, there are shots she could take."

That night before the Big Human left for work they decided. The Mother Human would take the Little Girl to a doctor as soon as she could get an appointment.

So a couple of days later, the Little Girl and her mother went to see the doctor. I stayed home with the sleeping grandmother. I slept a good bit, too. Nothing else to do.

Pretty soon, they were both home. The Little Girl was glad to see me, but the mother acted sort of strange. I had a bad feeling about this.

That night I heard the humans talking.

"The doctor believes she has severe allergies," the mother was saying. "He wants to do some tests, but he's pretty sure it's the cat."

"Lisa loves that cat," The Big Human said.

"Tell me about it."

"How about those shots Clarice mentioned; couldn't she get those?"

"I asked him. They're expensive."

"How expensive?"

"About a hundred dollars a shot. And she'd have to have one a week."

"Whoa! I don't think our insurance will cover that."

"It won't. I already checked."

"So much for union benefits."

"Wait, it gets worse. The doctor said if we don't do something right away, it could turn into asthma."

"Asthma!" the Big Human said. They went quiet for a while. Then he spoke. "I guess there's only one thing to do. I'm goin' to have to take the cat back where I found him."

"To that subway station? No, don't do that. Take him to the Humane Society or someplace."

"All right. I'll take him tomorrow morning after I get home. Do me a favor and look up some of those places in Manhattan. He might have a better chance there."

So, I was going to end up in one of those places after all.

Naturally, I was concerned about that. I had another feeling, too . . . one I didn't remember ever having it before. It had something to do with the Little Girl. But I'd think about that later.

Right now, I had to think of some way to escape. My prospects didn't look so good. I could try slipping out the window, of course. But it was a long way to the street. And even if I could make it to the street, I'd still be in Brooklyn. Who knows what they do to cats here?

I was still working on an escape plan when the Big Human came into the Little Girl's room. She was still sleeping when he lifted me off her bed and stuffed me in that Styrofoam box.

The Big Human didn't have much to say on the subway ride back to Manhattan. He just held the box with me inside. I didn't say much either.

It was still early morning when we got to the place where we had to change trains. It was already crowded with people rushing about. I could tell that, even if I couldn't actually see them.

I felt The Big Human set my box down. The lid wasn't on very tight, and I figured it was time to make my move. I jumped out of the box and ran for it.

I had to dodge feet right and left. All the humans were so intent on getting where they were going that they couldn't be bothered with a cat running for his life. I knew enough by then to stay away from the tracks. I headed in the direction of the fewest humans.

I zigged and zagged to avoid getting stepped on for

what seemed to be hours. Finally, I found some kind of counter to hide behind while I tried to catch my breath. As my breathing became more regular, I felt an old, familiar sensation. Hunger.

I'd been shoved in the box without breakfast.

I eased my way along a greasy, gray wall, trying to stay out of sight, while I tried to scope out my next meal. I slipped behind a rolling cart, and that's when I saw it. My next meal.

Even as hungry as I was, it didn't look that appetizing. From its smell, it hadn't been dead long, but I'd never eaten another animal before . . . dead or alive.

I'd never seen one of these before, either.

It was a rat.

I was working up my nerve to bite into it when I heard a voice.

"I wouldn't eat that if I were you."

I turned and saw another cat. An old cat. His fur was almost silver, and his eyes were soft and watery.

"I'm sorry," I said. "Is it yours?"

"Oh no," the Old Cat said. "I would never eat anything I find dead here. And I advise you not to—"

"Why is that?" I asked.

"Humans put out poison to kill these poor fellows. It seems they don't like rats very much. But the problem is, if a cat eats one of these poisoned rats, he gets killed, too."

"That's awful," I said.

"That's why you should never eat anything dead without asking yourself, How did it die? If you don't know, don't eat it."

"Thank you. I really didn't want to eat it very much. It's just that I'm so hungry."

"Hungry? My friend, you're in a food lover's paradise. There's plenty here to eat. American food . . . Mexican food . . . Jewish food . . . all kinds of food here at Grand

Central."

"So where is all this food?" I asked a little impatiently.

"Oh, you'll have to wait until things quiet down. There are too many humans around now. But later on tonight, you'll find plenty to eat. There's a great seafood place down on the lower level. And a food court, too."

"I don't know anything about this place," I said. "Only that it's noisy and full of trains and humans."

"Grand Central is warm and relatively safe. And you'll become accustomed to the crowds and the noise. Believe me, when winter comes, you'll thank the Great Cat you found your way to Grand Central."

"Are you the gray cat?" I asked.

"Gray cat? I don't understand."

"I thought you said something about a gray cat."

"You shouldn't make jokes about the Great Cat."

"I didn't mean to. It's just that I never heard of this Great Cat."

"You mean your mother never told you about the Great Cat when you were a kitten?"

"No, I guess she never got the chance. First thing I remember is being at a pet shop."

"Oh, that is such a shame. So many of our young cats are taken from their mothers at a tender age and never learn the Truths. It's no wonder some of them grow up to be wild and radical."

"Well, I'm neither. Until a few days ago, I had a human who took care of me. But she died."

"That's too bad," the Old Cat said. "But if you have no human, you must learn to rely on yourself. That is what the Great Cat teaches us."

"I'm learning pretty fast," I said. "But tell me, is that business about not eating dead things one of the Great Cat's teachings?"

"Oh no. That's just common sense."

The Old Cat and I exchanged names and talked for a while. Then he got up and stretched.

"You'll find that seafood place I mentioned if you go straight down this hallway. Good luck to you."

"Couldn't I just kind of hang out with you . . . until I get my bearings?" I wasn't sure I wanted to face this Grand Central place on my own.

"Oh no, that wouldn't do at all," the Old Cat said. "We're territorial, you know. Just find some territory of your own and mark it. You'll be fine."

The Old Cat was going to leave me to fend for myself. I had to think fast.

"But I want to know more about the Great Cat," I said. "If you don't tell me, nobody will."

The Old Cat stopped and stroked his whiskers.

"I'm sorry, my son. But I'm really too old to be taking on a new disciple."

"I won't be any trouble . . . I promise. And there's so much I want to know."

I knew I was sounding desperate. I *was* desperate.

"Well, I suppose I could take you on for a little while. Maybe you could run a few errands for me, too. It's getting hard for me to get up those steps. Arthritis, you know."

I thanked the Old Cat over and over until he told me to stop.

I was hoping we'd go to one of those places the Old Cat had mentioned, so I could eat. Instead, I followed him to his place—a neat little tunnel in the wall—where were to begin my lessons.

Over the next few hours, the Old Cat droned on about the Great Cat. He claimed that most of the things we cats do were the Great Cat's idea—everything from washing our faces after we eat to burying our . . . well . . . you know. He explained why dogs are our sworn enemies. He told me why we always land on our feet and like to climb things.

He told me a lot of other stuff, but I was so hungry it was hard to concentrate.

Finally, he stopped talking about the Great Cat and got around to a subject I really cared about. Food.

As I followed him down a dark hallway, I could already smell the delightful aroma of fresh fish. I had to force myself not to shove the Old Cat aside and make a beeline to the source of that aroma.

Apparently, I wasn't the only cat in Grand Central that felt that way. When we finally got to the alleyway behind the seafood place, I could see it was packed with cats.

I figured we were out of luck. But the Old Cat cleared his throat and spoke. "Brothers and sisters, welcome your new brother to whom I have given the name Azmuel which means seeker. Let us share with him in our bounty."

Then he said, "The Great Cat be with you."

"And also with you," the cats replied.

Then, the crowd of cats parted and let us pass. The cats bowed respectfully to the Old Cat, but they didn't look any too pleased to see me. At any rate, we got first shot at the fish. And they were delicious.

This was going to be sweet, I thought. All I'd have to do was pretend to be interested in this Great Cat stuff, and I'd have a roof over my head and eat like a king.

At least, that's what I thought.

Being a disciple got old fast.

It was bad enough that I had to listen to the Old Cat ramble on all day about this Great Cat; he expected me to be his servant.

So every day I'd have to go to passageways behind the

seafood place or the food court and bring the Old Cat his meals. The other cats knew I was working for the Old One, so they let me take what I wanted, but I could tell they didn't like it. Or me.

Trouble was, by the time the Old Cat was through gumming his food, there wasn't much left for me. And if I went back to get my own, the good food would be all gone.

But that wasn't the half of it. The Old Cat expected me to groom him after every meal.

That meant licking his dusty fur and getting hair all in my mouth. Meanwhile, my own coat was getting more and more beat-up looking. Without somebody to brush me every day, I was beginning to look like an anarchist's cat.

The Old Cat paid no attention to me, of course. He just kept on and on about the Great Cat. I couldn't really ask him questions. He was as deaf as a post—that's why he didn't mind the noise at Grand Central. He could read lips—but only if he was looking in your direction. Most of the time he didn't look in mine. He just talked.

I never understood exactly where this Great Cat lived or anything. All I got was a bunch of rules about how he expected us to behave.

Some of the rules made sense. Like treating other cats the way you'd want them to treat you. Others just seemed stupid.

I put up with the Old Cat and his preaching for as long as I could. I just couldn't take the noise of this place and the crowds of humans tromping through. So after maybe a month of that, I finally got the Old Cat's attention.

"Teacher," I said. "I think I'm ready."

"Ready for what . . . er . . . Azmuel?" He was always forgetting the name he had given me.

"Ready to go back out into the world. And I wanted to thank you for teaching me about the Great Cat."

"But you don't know half there is to know! We've

hardly begun your instruction."

"No, you've done a much better job than you realize. I've learned a lot, and I know the Great Cat himself would be proud of you."

"If you leave this place now, Azmuel, you may never find your way back. And I am old. I may not be here, even if you did."

"That would sadden me, Teacher. But I'm sure you'll live for many a year to come . . . if the Great Cat wills it."

I surprised myself—I was beginning to sound like I believed this stuff.

Finally, the Old Cat agreed that I should go. But he didn't like it much. I guess he wasn't looking forward to getting his own food.

I spent the remainder of the day resting, getting ready to hit the streets. I figured my chances were better at night, so I planned to leave then.

It was hard to tell whether it was day or night in that place. Gradually, the trains and the humans became less numerous, and I figured it was late.

I stopped by the Old Cat's cave to say good-bye. But he appeared to be asleep. I had a funny feeling about leaving him . . . couldn't really say what it was or why I felt it. But my mind was made up. All I had to do now was to find my way out of the place.

That was harder than you'd think, and it took a long time. They were closing the doors when I scooted out into the cool night air.

I was on the street again.

Chapter Nine. Madison Avenue.
I Learn that Revenge Is a Thick, Juicy Steak.

I won't bore you with all the details of my life after I left Grand Central. It was mostly, look for something to eat . . . look for a place to sleep . . . look for something to eat.

Who am I kidding? It was all about looking for food. I was hungry all the time. And I'd never been hungry—I mean really hungry . . . before. Sometimes the humans who worked at restaurants and pizza places would toss me a few scraps. But they never invited me inside.

I got to be fairly good at finding stuff in garbage cans. Perfectly good food people had thrown out. OK, so some of it wasn't perfectly good. But if you're hungry enough, pretty soon it doesn't matter.

I also learned how to cross streets without getting run over. I'd wait until a human was crossing. Then when he'd step off the curb, I'd run like crazy.

I still didn't like crossing very much, though, and never tried it again on the big wide streets. Like Park Avenue. Forget about it.

Every once in a while I'd see my reflection in a glass door. I looked awful. My long, black hair was all matted from being wet and dirty and not being brushed.

It wasn't even like hair anymore. It was stiff and hard. Like armor. I didn't look like a cat at all. I looked like . . . an armadillo. I'd seen them on the nature programs the Old Lady used to watch, and that's what I looked like. Only black.

There was one good thing about the way I looked, though. I didn't have much trouble with other cats or even dogs. One look at me, and they'd generally cross to the other side of the street.

Of course, the downside of that was most humans would, too.

I was pretty sure no human would ever take me home—not with me looking like some monster that had crawled out of the sewer. I figured I was on my own for good.

I'd never really been all alone before. Closest I ever came to that was when the Old Lady would go to the opera or the theater and leave me at home. But I always knew she'd come back. She'd sit with me on her lap for hours and tell me all about the opera or the play she'd seen. I sort of missed that.

Once and awhile, I'd pass a store and see a cat in the window. Inside where it was safe and dry.

I envied those cats.

One night I was walking down the street, looking for food as usual. Except that I was hungrier than usual. I hadn't had a decent meal in days. I was passing an alley, when I got a whiff of a pleasant aroma. Steak! I was so hungry that I plowed straight into that alley.

Right into a gang of cats. The same gang that had left me to die in the subway.

It was different this time. The cats took one look at me and cringed back against the wall. They didn't recognize me.

"We don't want any trouble," one of the cats said in a shaky voice.

"Then hand over that steak, and there won't be any," I said, trying to sound as much like Clint Eastwood as it was possible for a cat.

"Sure . . . sure . . . take what you want . . . just leave us alone," the cat said.

I turned to leave with the piece of steak in my mouth, when I heard a vaguely familiar voice.

"What goes on here?"

It was the cat they called the Skipper.

"This monster is taking the steak, Skip."

The cat called the Skipper took a long, hard look at me and then smiled.

"No, youse is mistaken, Guido. This . . . er . . . cat is a guest of ours. I invited him here to share our steak."

The cats all looked at one another.

"So back off and let me have a private word with our guest."

The cats stepped back into the shadows, but I could feel their eyes on us. The Skipper cat came up close and spoke to me in a soft voice.

"Look, you're making me look bad in front of my crew. Take a couple more bites and leave the rest of the steak, OK?"

"I guess you didn't understand me. I'm taking this steak. All of it."

I was getting carried away with this Clint Eastwood thing. The steak really was too big to take. I would have to drag it all over the filthy sidewalk. But I didn't see how I could back down now.

Fortunately, I didn't have to. The Skipper cat looked over his shoulder at his gang and whispered in my ear.

"You know, I could use a big cat like you in our organization. If you're not otherwise affiliated . . ."

I just looked at him, the steak still in my mouth.

"You could be my Number Two. You'd get first dibs on everything—after me of course."

"No thanks," I told him. "I work alone."

With that I left. As I cleared the alley, I could hear an awful ruckus behind me. Sounded like a huge cat fight. I figured the Skipper had just lost his crew.

I headed for my spot under some steps to finish my steak.

I never enjoyed a meal more.

Chapter Ten. Central Park.
I Become Sick and Nearly a Hawk's Breakfast.

I'm not real good at telling time. So I have no idea how long I'd been on my own. Weeks . . . months . . . who knows?

It had been nice and cool when I first hit the streets. Comfortable. Then it started getting hot. Really hot. And me wearing a fur coat.

Our apartment had been air conditioned. The streets weren't. I was always thirsty. Nobody ever thinks to put water out for cats.

But now I could feel a change in the air. It didn't feel like air conditioning. It was more like when the Old Lady would open the refrigerator to give me dinner. Except this time I didn't expect to be getting anything to eat. Unless it was from a garbage can.

I guess you can eat out of them for only so long before it catches up with you.

I was feeling sick. Real sick.

I'd had a few fur balls in my day, but this was nothing like it. I felt achy and hot all over. Then I'd feel like I had a ringside seat in a freezer.

Since there was nobody to take me to the vet, I'd have to handle this on my own. I remembered what the Old Cat had said:

"When you feel sick, eat some grass."

I couldn't recall if it was from the teachings of the Great Cat or if the Old Cat had come up with that one on his own. But I figured it was worth a shot.

Only problem was finding grass growing in Manhattan. I remembered going through a big park with the Old Lady in her car. I couldn't remember the name of it, but I thought it might be west of here. I'd just keep heading west until I found it.

It was early in the morning, and I guess it must have been a Sunday because there wasn't much traffic on the streets. That was a good thing since I didn't feel like running or dodging cars.

I kept on walking west for blocks until I could see what looked like a park across the street from some apartment buildings. I waited for a break in traffic and then ran across as fast as I was able. When I got to the other side, I noticed a bunch of humans on the sidewalk I'd just come from. They were all looking up at one of the buildings. Some of them had cameras; others were using binoculars or cell phones.

Whatever it was they were gawking at didn't concern me. I had grass to find. I made my way through an iron railing fence and started looking for some. I could see that I was going to have to go farther into the park if I was going to find grass that humans hadn't walked on and dogs had left alone.

I spotted what appeared to be a decent clump of grass

sort of out in the open and was making my way toward
it when I heard the humans shouting. I was just about to
chow down on a few choice blades when I sensed something terrible was about to happen.

I just had time to jerk my head up when I saw this huge,
black shadow right above my head. I was too startled to run,
and by the time I'd gathered my wits the thing was on me.

His claws were digging into my back—or would have
been if my fur hadn't been so thick and matted. But, at any
rate, he was trying to pick me up.

"Hey! The hawk has got a little dog!" I heard somebody
yell.

It took a second for me to realize he was yelling about
me. I was certainly no dog. But the thing definitely had me
and was trying his best to fly off with me. It was flapping
its wings like crazy, but it couldn't quite lift me off the
ground.

But I couldn't shake him off either. I knew I had to do
something fast before he got enough momentum to lift me.
I spotted a bench and headed toward it.

The thing saw what I was trying to do and was trying
to get his claws loose. I figured I'd help him and ran under
the bench. The impact knocked the thing loose. Without
looking back, he flew away—toward the street.

I planned to stay under the bench until I was sure he
was gone. Some humans ran over and one said, "Hey, it
wasn't a dog. This is a cat!"

"How about that? Bird catches cat!" another human
said. He seemed to think it was funny. I didn't see much
humor in it.

Some of the humans called to me, but I stayed put.
Eventually, they got bored and moved on. So did I. I found
a little tunnel and stayed there for the rest of the day only
venturing out long enough to grab a quick bite of grass
from the patch growing next to it.

I must have dozed off. I woke up when I heard voices.

"It's gotta be him."

It was a female human.

Two of them were crouching down and peering into the tunnel.

"It's a sign, I tell you," one of the females was saying. "A great bird . . . a black cat . . . it has to be."

"C'mon kitty," the other was calling to me. There were two of them, human females. From what I could see, they looked harmless enough, so I moved slowly toward them.

"He's perfect!" one of them said. "I knew he would be when I heard about the hawk and him on the radio."

The other one had lifted me and was holding me up so they both could take a look. And I could see both of them. They were young females, dressed in black. One had all sorts of metal things in her face which must have hurt something awful; the other didn't. She just looked pale.

Both of them had very black hair and very black lipstick.

"I don't know, Tish . . . We wanted a black cat, but I had sort of pictured one with short hair. And the hair on this one . . ." She trailed off as if she didn't know what to say.

"No, this is just what we want. See how fierce he looks. And feel his hair . . . it's hard and stiff . . . like some sort of prehistoric reptile."

"Don't rub it in," I thought to myself.

"He'll be the perfect familiar," the female called Tish was saying.

"A familiar?" Just what the heck was a "familiar," I wondered.

The females had brought a box with holes in it, but it was much too small. So they took turns holding me on the subway.

"This cat is sick," one of them said.

"Even better," the other one said. "It'll give us the chance to try out the spells."

Chapter Eleven. West 4th Street.
I Am Taken in by Witches of the West Village.

I was really feeling awful by the time we got to the place the females lived. It was above a shop of some kind and in a part of town I had never been to. They wrapped me in a nice, warm towel, and one of them got busy boiling something on the stove. It smelled terrible.

"Here kitty, drink this." Was she kidding? No way I was going to drink something that smelled that bad.

"It's for your own good," the one called Nina said. She grabbed me and put her fingers in the corners of my mouth, forcing it open. The other one emptied a spoonful of the terrible smelling stuff in my mouth.

I did what any normal cat would do. I spat it out.

They tried that a couple of times with the same results. Finally, they gave up and decided to fix me a bowl of food. Only it wasn't like any food I had ever seen before. It was like twigs and leaves. I was plenty hungry, but I couldn't eat that stuff.

"He won't eat this," Nina said, stating the obvious. "I'll go out and get some real cat food. We'll put the herb potion in that."

"You're not bringing meat in here!" Tish said. She seemed alarmed.

"No, of course not. I'll get some dry cat food."

The one called Nina went out to get me some food, while the other one stood over me and sang a peculiar song. I couldn't make out the words; they were in a language I didn't know.

Eventually, Nina came back with some store-brand dry food. I didn't feel much like eating, but I didn't know when I might get the chance to eat again, so I tried. The food wasn't very good; it was kind of stale, and they made it worse by pouring some of that terrible stuff over it. But I ate as much of it as I could.

Next morning, I felt even worse. I felt like I was going to die.

"He's no better," Tish said. "I believe he's worse."

"We should take him to a veterinarian," Nina said.

"A veterinarian!" Tish shouted. "Are you crazy? We can't take him to a veterinarian. We're witches!"

"Witches?" I'd heard the word someplace, but I didn't know what it meant. I had a feeling it wasn't anything good.

As the day went on, they tried a bunch of different potions on my food. They rubbed some kind of foul-smelling stuff all over my back. Nothing seemed to help.

"I'm going to take him to a veterinarian," Nina said. "They can kick me out of the coven if they want, but I'm not going to let an innocent animal suffer."

"You can't go back on your oath just because of a sick cat," Tish said. "What kind of witch are you, anyway?"

"I'm the kind who pays the rent around here," she shot back.

"Oh, you're going to bring that up again, are you? Well, you're the one with the trust fund . . . the one who thinks witchcraft is just some kind of game . . . the one who—"

"The one who took you in . . ." Nina broke in. "The only one who'd have you!"

"That's it—I'm not staying here a minute longer. I'll send for my things."

"What things? You don't even own the shirt on your back—it happens to be mine!"

With that, the one called Tish stormed out the door and slammed it hard. The minute she did, Nina rushed into the bedroom and came back with a large, black handbag. She rummaged around in it and brought out a bottle, unscrewed the top, and fished out a capsule, which she proceeded to take apart. Then she poured the powder inside over a fresh bowl of cat food.

The dry cat food wasn't the best I ever had, but I managed to get most of it down. There was kind of an aftertaste, which I guessed was from the stuff she had poured over it. I went to sleep after that and must have slept most of the day. When I woke up it was dark. I had some more food with pill powder in it and some water. Then I went back to sleep.

Next day, I woke up feeling like a new cat. No more chills, no more feeling hot all over. And was I hungry!

The female could tell right away that I was better. Since I'd eaten most of the cat food she'd bought the day before, she said she'd go to the store for more.

"You stay here, and I'll be right back."

She'd only been gone for a little while when I heard the

sound of a key in the door. I figured it was Nina with my food, so I stood up.

But I was wrong. It was the other one. Tish.

"Who does she think she is? To throw me out without a dime." She was talking to herself. She came into the bedroom and saw me.

"I'm just taking what's mine," she said, reaching into Nina's handbag.

"Hah, what's this?" She was holding up the bottle of medicine.

"I knew it—I knew it!" she said.

She put the bottle in her pocket and went back out the door, locking it from the other side. A few minutes later I heard another key in the door. This time it was Nina with my cat food.

She put the bag down and said, "OK, chow time."

She poured a some food in the bowl that had become mine and disappeared into the bedroom. She came right out.

"That's weird. The bottle of antibiotics . . . it's missing."

She was about to say something else but stopped. There was the sound of a key in the door again.

It was Tish. And she had some other females with her. I didn't like the look of them. They were all dressed in black, and they seemed really mad about something. I hopped down, ran back into the bedroom, and hid under the bed.

One of the mad females had the bottle that had held the medicine Nina had given me. She held it up close to Nina's face. Nina just stood there without moving.

"Look at this, Nina. It's from a doctor. It's for a 'Nina Krelstein.' And it's dated a month ago. You were taking the Others' medicines, after you took the oath!"

"Some witch you turned out to be," one of the others said.

"What are you people doing in my apartment?" Nina said coldly. "I don't recall inviting you in."

"Nina Krelstein, you are a disgrace to your coven and to witchcraft!" the female with the bottle screeched. "You will appear tonight before the entire coven to be judged."

"And you'll leave my medicine right here," Nina shot back.

The angry witch threw down the bottle. I was surprised it didn't break. Plastic, I suppose.

Then the angry witch put her face right up into Nina's and said, "Bring the cat."

Bring the cat? that didn't sound like much of an invitation. In fact, it sounded downright scary.

Nina didn't say much the rest of the day. She just smoked cigarettes and drank a lot of red wine. Cigarette smoke isn't good for cats, so I perched on a window sill and watched people go by.

After a long time, she came into the bedroom and threw some clothes in a duffel bag. Then she got dressed, not in the same black outfit I'd seen her in before but one that looked all new. It was like she was going out for something special.

"C'mon cat," she said. "It's show time."

I wasn't all that eager to go, but I went anyway. I had a bad feeling about this.

We walked for a couple of blocks, Nina holding me but saying nothing. We came to another building like hers and walked up a flight of stairs. Nina took a deep breath and opened the door.

The room was full of human females, all dressed in black. There was a table at one end of the room with candles on each end. In the middle was something I'd only seen on TV and never counted on seeing in real life.

It was a human skull, all white and shiny as if it had just been polished. The angry witch—the one who'd come to the apartment—walked to the front of the room and stood behind the table. I guessed that she was the head witch.

She said some words in a language I couldn't understand. Then the other witches repeated the words. Then they sang a kind of low, mournful song that seemed to go on forever. Then more words, more mournful song.

I was getting bored and tried to get down, but Nina was holding me tight.

Finally, the head witch said, "Bring the erring sister forward."

Two of the witches shoved Nina and me toward the table. The head witch nodded to one of them, and she took me from Nina's arms.

"Bind the cat," the head witch said.

With that, they took long black cords and tied me to the table. They had moved the skull over to the edge to make room for me, but I could still see it, and it didn't help my nerves.

"Erring sister!" the head witch said loudly. "You are one of our newest. And you have been a great benefactor to the coven over the past few months. Accordingly, if you but confess your transgressions against the Dark Lord and beg his forgiveness and ours, you may yet be spared."

"Yes, my sisters, I have transgressed. I saw a doctor for my sinus infection, and I took the medicine he gave me," Nina said.

"Do you confess doing this after you had taken a blood oath to the Dark Lord?" the head witch asked.

"Yes," Nina said quietly. She hung her head down, as if she were truly sorry.

The witches gasped.

"She must pay!" one of them shouted. The others seemed to agree with that.

"Erring sister, you have confessed to your wrongful deeds," the head witch said.

"Now there is a task you must perform if you are to be redeemed."

She reached behind the table and brought up a large sword. The witches oohed and ahhed at that.

"You must perform the sacrificial rite," the witch said, holding the sword high above her head.

"You must kill the cat!"

Kill the cat? I didn't sign up for that. I wriggled as hard as I could, but the cords were tightly tied.

"Surely, sister," Nina said quietly. "Give me the sword."

Nina seemed to be in a trance. She was really going to do it!

The head witch handed Nina the sword. She held above her head and right over me. I closed my eyes. I didn't want to see this.

"Sister," Nina said to the head witch. "He's moving about so. Could you perhaps tie the bonds a little tighter?"

The head witch reached down to make my already tight cords even tighter. What was this Nina human thinking?

As she bent down, Nina threw her arm around the head witch's neck and brought her up straight. She had a chokehold on the witch with one arm and was holding the sword with her other hand. The witches were stunned.

"All right, you skags. Nobody moves. Except you two. Untie the cat."

The two witches did, and I jumped to the floor.

"Now, listen!" Nina was shouting to the witches.

"You call yourselves 'witches'—you're nothing but a pathetic bunch of losers . . . dressing up like everyday was Halloween and playing your stupid games."

She paused to take a breath.

"Well, I've had enough of you and your 'Dark Lord.' Playing 'witch' is one thing, but when you try to hurt an innocent animal who's done nothing to you—that's it. I'm going home—and back to Bryn Mawr."

Nina released her grip on the head witch and shoved her aside. The witch coughed for a bit but was finally able to speak.

"You are doomed! Doomed, I say! The Dark Lord will follow you to the ends of the earth and will punish you!"

"Oh, I think your Dark Lord is going to be much too busy to do that—too busy putting out the fire!"

She swung the sword and knocked both lighted candles onto the floor. The cloth around the table burst into flames.

"C'mon cat," she said to me. "Let's get out of here."

The witches were rushing to get water from the kitchen and trying to put out the fire. They were too busy to try to stop us. When we got to the street, Nina turned to me, "Guess that martial arts course paid off, huh?"

She looked up at the second-story window.

"Looks like they have it under control. But just to be sure . . ."

Nina dialed 911 on her cell phone and reported a fire at the address we'd just left. Then we walked back to her apartment.

We only stayed long enough for Nina to change out of the black outfit and into a sweatshirt and jeans, grab the bag she had packed, and write a note to the landlord. Then we hopped in a cab and headed for the Port Authority Bus Station.

Nina bought a one-way ticket to a place called

Philadelphia, but when we tried to board the bus, they wouldn't let me on. They said I had to be in a cage, and there were no cat-carrier stores open at that hour.

So we said good-bye in front of the Port Authority.

"Cat, we weren't together long enough for me to even give you a name," she said. "But you helped me see that whole witch-thing for what it is. I thought it was like Wicca. You know, about nature and stuff. Who knew about that "Dark Lord" thing?"

I just sat there on the sidewalk, looking up at her.

"I wish I could take you with me, but I can't. You understand . . . don't you?"

I understood, all right.

She was going back to her family, and I was going back to the street.

Chapter Twelve. East 29th Street.
I Am Warned of Danger by a Ghostly Cat.

I didn't know this part of town at all.

One thing was for sure. I wanted to avoid those witches. They'd be sore because Nina had spoiled their little ceremony and they'd take it out on me. So just to be on the safe side, I decided to head north for a while and then work my way east. But that didn't work—too many humans. I was forced to zig and zag.

I must have walked for hours before admitting to myself that I was lost. I know, cats are supposed to have an excellent sense of direction and ordinarily I do. But after what I'd just been through, you couldn't blame me for being a little off my game.

It was almost time for the sun to come up, and that meant a lot of humans on the streets. That was always dangerous for cats, so I started looking for a place to hole up until it was safe to travel again.

Funny thing about New York. Most people think it's just tall buildings and swanky apartments like the one I used to live in. But there are also a lot of beat-up-looking buildings.

I happened to be passing by one of those, and I stopped to consider it. Before the giant bird incident, I'd been sleeping under a dumpster next to a dry-cleaning plant. It was on concrete blocks, so there was room for me, and it seemed safe enough. But the fumes from the dry cleaners had been giving me a headache lately, and I was in the market for a new place. Maybe this one.

There was a sign on the building, but I don't read too well, so I ignored it and looked for a way in. Pretty soon I found a window that had been boarded up but had a few missing planks. I hopped through the open space.

You can usually tell if there's nobody else in a building. I immediately knew I was all alone in this one. There didn't even seem to be any mice, which was odd.

This had once been somebody's home. A long time ago, I guessed. The ceilings were high, and there were marble fireplaces just like my old place. The walls had cracks in them; there was dust and trash everywhere, and some of the wooden flooring was missing. There was a faint human smell, as if some of them had spent some time here but had moved on.

I took a look upstairs and found a small room. There were some rags on the floor that didn't smell too bad, so I settled down in them.

I'd had a trying night, what with witches trying to kill me and all, so I fell asleep right away. I must have really been tired because I didn't wake up until really late in the morning. I stretched and then went out the window in search of something to eat.

People in this part of town seemed a lot more generous

than where I'd been living. There was a pizza place that was always good for a crust or two. And although I wasn't crazy about Chinese food, I could count on some scraps at one of those places.

This wasn't bad, I thought. I had a good, safe place to sleep and was eating decent food on a fairly regular basis. I'd been in this neighborhood for a couple of weeks and figured maybe I'd settle down here.

It was really late when I got back to my room. I'd had a particularly busy night scavenging for food, so I fell asleep right away.

I awoke with a start.

There was something else in the room. I could sense it before I could see it.

And when I saw it, I didn't believe my eyes.

It was another cat. But not like any cat I'd ever seen before. He seemed to glow faintly like the screen of an old TV set that's just been turned off.

There was something else odd about him. I could see through him. I could see the wall behind him as if he had been made of glass. I thought I was dreaming and shook my head. But the cat was still there.

He looked in my direction and spoke to me in Cat.

"Get out!" was what he said.

I closed my eyes for a second, and the see-through cat was gone. I got up and smelled the place he'd been standing. No scent at all. It was as if he'd never been there. I kept telling myself it had just been a dream. Still, I had a lot of trouble getting back to sleep.

The next day was pretty much like all the others. I

scavenged and begged for food and tried to stay out of humans' way. But, to tell the truth, I couldn't shake that dream.

That night I dreaded going to sleep for fear I'd have it again.

But eventually I fell asleep. And just like the night before, I woke up and saw the cat.

Again, he spoke to me in Cat and told me to get out. But this time, he called me by name.

I knew I had to be dreaming. Nobody had called me by my real name in a long time. Somehow, I managed to fall asleep again, and when I awoke the sun was shining through the cracks in the boarded-up windows. I went about my routine and tried not to think of the see-through cat.

But I couldn't help thinking about him.

What kind of cat could he be? And why was he telling me to get out of the best place I'd found? I was still asking myself those questions that night when I drifted off to sleep.

"GET OUT!" This time it was the cat's voice that woke me. I opened my eyes to see he wasn't all the way across the room, the way he'd been before. He was practically in my face.

"W . . . hh . . . y?" I tried to ask him, but I was too scared to even form the words.

"GET OUT NOW!" The cat was practically screaming. Then he vanished . . . right before my eyes.

There was no way I was going back to sleep after that. I just lay there—shivering with fear.

I lay there until I felt the building start to shake.

I had no idea what was going on. The whole building was shaking. Then there'd be a pause, and it would shake again. It was like somebody was pounding on it with a huge hammer—taking a short break between swings.

I had seen programs about earthquakes on the Old Lady's TV, so I guessed that's what was going on. I didn't know we had earthquakes in Manhattan, but I'd learned there was a lot I didn't know.

BOOM! That hammer again. Dust came flying from the walls. I expected they would give way any minute, so I decided to head for someplace safer. I ran downstairs.

I figured the basement would be the safest place, so I started looking for a way down there. There was a doorway I hadn't seen before. I guessed the earthquake had jarred the door open.

BOOM! I ran down the stairs as fast as I could. It was dark in the basement and hard to see anything—even for a cat.

Gradually, my eyes became accustomed to the dark, and I made my way over to a wall that seemed farthest from where the booming was coming from. I squeezed up against the wall and closed my eyes as tight as I could and waited for the earthquake to be over.

The next sound I heard made the booming sound like a kid with a drum. This was no boom. It was a roar—like the walls upstairs were coming down. The floor over my head shook—dust poured down . . . and then the floor gave way.

Everything happened at once. Bricks . . . wood . . . metal, and it was all coming my way. Somehow I managed to look up, and for an instant I saw the sky. Then I saw nothing at all.

I must have gotten knocked out, because the next thing I knew I was under some heavy pieces of wood. I was totally pinned down and couldn't move at all. I could barely breathe—it was if all the air had been knocked out of my lungs and replaced by dust.

I'm not sure how long I lay there . . . I kept blacking

out. I felt like I'd had a wall dropped on me . . . which, in fact, was precisely what had happened.

The next thing I remember was some human shouting "Hey! There's something under here! A dog or cat or something."

A couple of big humans pulled the heavy wood off me, and I struggled to get to my feet.

"It's a cat," one of them said. "Take it easy, cat. I got you." That reminded me of something that had happened to me before, but I couldn't think what. Next thing I knew the human had picked me up in his arms and was telling another one to call Animal Control.

Animal Control was the last thing I wanted to hear, but I was too out of it to try and get away. I'd just have to let whatever was going to happen happen.

I was able to look around a little, expecting to see damage all over the place. But it was just this one building . . . the one where I'd spent the night. All the rest were OK.

I could see a huge machine with an iron ball on a chain. That thing was what had knocked down my building . . . not an earthquake.

I couldn't imagine why they'd go to all that trouble just to evict a cat.

Chapter Thirteen. East 110th Street.
I Am Delivered into the Hands of My Enemies.

I guess I blacked out again, because when I came to I was on a cold metal slab with a bunch of white-coated humans bending over me. I tried to move, but there were rubber straps holding me down.

"Let's see if there are any broken bones before we do anything else," one of the humans was saying. Somebody moved a big thing like a camera over me, and they all stepped behind a wall.

When they came out, they crowded around a TV screen. I tried to turn my head so I could see too, but they had me tied down pretty good.

"Well, no bones that I can see, and the internals look OK. Probably just some bruising on the shoulders," the human said. He sounded like he was in charge of things.

"His temp is a little elevated," a female human said. "But he may have been sick before the building came down on him."

"Probably dehydrated. Put him on a drip and hit him

with a round of amoxicillin, just in case he's picked up a bug. Once we get this hair off him, I'll do a proper exam."

One of the humans took some kind of buzzing thing and shaved off a patch of my fur in back. I could feel a pinprick on that spot. I closed my eyes, but I could hear the humans talking.

"I've never seen a cat with hair like this. Feel how hard it is across the back. I didn't think I could get enough off for the IV."

"Persian, I'm guessing," the female said. "They matt up pretty quick when there's nobody to take care of them. No telling how long this one's been out on the streets."

She paused for a minute. "No sign of a collar. And he's been neutered. Do we have a scanner that's working?"

"Both of them still out. Probably wouldn't work through all this fur anyway."

"Could you bring up his x-ray again?" she asked. The other human turned on the computer.

They stared at the screen.

"There's something there. See over by the shoulder. Might be a chip."

"Anyway, we're going to have to shave this fur off. No way we can comb all this out."

"I'm guessing we'll have to put him under, and he's too weak for that now."

Put him under! I didn't like the sound of that. But I'd worry about that later.

Right now, I just wanted to sleep.

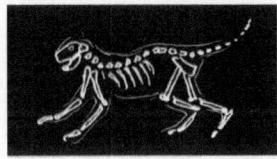

When I woke up, I was in another room. Whatever they'd attached to my back seemed to be gone, and I wasn't tied down anymore. I was, however, in a small cage. I had no idea how long I'd been out.

"Swell treatment, huh?" It was a cat in the next cage.

I answered him with a question of my own.

"What is this place?"

"Animal Control," the other cat said. "The place where cats like us end up."

"What do you mean 'end up'?"

"It's like the roach motel for cats. We checked in but we won't be checking out."

I didn't understand. The other cat made it clear.

"We've got a one-way ticket to that big catnip patch in the sky," the cat said.

"You mean they're going to?—"

"Fraid so, kid. It's the Big Sleep for us."

"What would make them want to . . . do that . . . to us?" I asked.

"Can't say for you. But me, I bite humans. I bite 'em every chance I get. That's why they call me Monster."

"You bite them? Why?"

"It's my way of getting back at 'em for what they've done to us. The way they hold us down."

I knew what that was like, having only recently been held down by witches and the people in white coats.

"A wise old cat told me all about it once," Monster was saying. "He said that cats once ruled the world. There was this great cat empire that stretched from Abyssinia to Siam, and it was all ruled by a cat emperor in a place called Katmandu."

I didn't see how cats could rule the world if we couldn't even operate a can opener, but I didn't want to get into an argument with Monster. It was the first real conversation I'd had in a long time.

"There was even a special class of humans called cat servants, and they waited on us paw and paw. Then one day, they decided they'd had enough and formed an alliance with the dogs. They rose up against us, and it's been nothing but misery for us cats ever since."

The cat called Monster went quiet for a while. Then he asked softly, "What did they say when they examined you?"

"Something about putting me under. Do you know what that means?"

"Yeah, I'm sorry, kid. It's human for exterminate with extreme prejudice."

"I thought they wanted to help me get well."

"That's just what they want you to think. They want to give you a false sense of security, so you won't resist."

"But they gave me some stuff they said would help me."

"Probably left over from one of their fiendish medical experiments. That's what they use some of us for. Those cats are the real unlucky ones."

I didn't say anything for a while. Neither did Monster. Then he whispered, "Listen kid. You and me, we got nothing to lose, right?"

I agreed. It certainly seemed that way.

"Then what do you say we go down fighting? We won't go to meet the Great Cat without doing some serious damage. With me?"

"Sure, but how? I'm not much of a fighter."

"You don't have to be. Just a decent actor. When they come for you, you pretend to have taken a turn for the worse, right? All curled up at the other end of the cage."

"OK, I guess I can do that."

"See, I've been working on this cage door, and I've got it pretty loose. The minute the human leans over and reaches in your cage, I'll jump on his back. You run out of the cage and head for the door."

"What then?" I asked.

"I'm going to try and free these other cats. Solidarity, right?"

"Maybe I should stay and try to help you," I said.

"No, you split for outside. They'll chase you, and that'll keep them out of here for a few minutes."

"Now, listen carefully," Monster said. "When you get to the street, turn right and head east toward the river. There's a raised highway that runs beside it. Wait under that highway till I get there. We'll meet some cats who'll help us. My FLF brothers."

"FLF?" I asked.

"Feline Liberation Front. We're gonna take back what's rightfully ours. We're gonna free cats everywhere. Are you with me on this?"

"Sure," I answered. Like Monster said, I didn't have a lot to lose.

We talked for a while and told each other our cat names. He wanted to be called Monster instead of his real name. It was his "nom de guerre" or war name, he said.

We talked a little more, and I asked him if he really believed in all that stuff about the Great Cat.

"Of course," he said. "I may be militant, but I'm no atheist."

I was a little embarrassed to talk about it—I was afraid he'd think I was weird. But I decided to tell Monster about the see-through cat. He didn't think it was strange at all.

"Could have been a spirit messenger from the other side," he said. "Or the ghost of some cat who'd died in that house."

He went quiet for a moment, as if he was thinking. Then he spoke again.

"But most likely it was some part of your brain telling you there was something odd about a place that the mice had abandoned and that maybe you should, too."

I thought about that for a while. Then I told him about the Old Lady dying, but that didn't make a big impression.

Monster didn't like humans at all.

Chapter Fourteen. York Avenue.
I Become a Fugitive.

For a long time, I thought they were going to leave us there all night without anything to eat or drink. And I was starving.

After a while, the door opened and a human came through it with a cart. He was a skinny human and was wearing a thick wool sweater. On his cart were bowls of dry cat food and little bowls of water.

"OK, this is it," Monster whispered. "Go into your act."

I was beginning to have second thoughts about this. I was awfully hungry and that cat food looked mighty good, even though it was probably store brand. But I couldn't let Monster down.

So I curled up at the far end of the cage and started meowing like I was dying. The skinny human came over to my cage and looked through the door.

"What's the matter, buddy? You not feeling so good?"

I yowled and moaned something awful. I could hear him opening my cage door.

"OK, big fellow. Let's see . . . YEOW!!!"

In a flash, Monster was on the human's back, his claws digging into the poor fellow. Or at least they would have been if the human hadn't been wearing such a heavy sweater.

"RUN FOR IT!" Monster was yelling at the top of his voice all the while holding onto the human.

I jumped down from the cage and onto the floor. Just then, there was a terrible crash as the human went down with Monster on his back. On his way down, he knocked over a couple of cages. The cats inside ran out through the open cage doors. I did what Monster had told me to do and headed straight for the door. I put all my weight against it, and it flew open. The cats and I ran through it. Looking back over my shoulder, I could see Monster struggling to open another cage.

We ran through kind of a lobby. And up to a big door. It was closed, and there was no way I could open it. The other cats were no help. They were yowling and mewling and making no sense at all.

It looked as if our Great Escape was going to be a flop. Just then the door opened. A male human in a suit stood there in the doorway like he didn't know what to make of all that was going on. That was all we needed for our getaway.

I didn't see what happened to the other cats. They were long gone before I got to the street. So much for solidarity.

I headed east toward the river like I'd been told to do. Every once in a while I'd stop and look back, but I didn't see Monster anywhere.

I didn't see any FLF members either, so I found a place under the highway next to a big stone column and waited.

And while I was waiting, I thought about what Monster had said.

The more I thought about it, the surer I was that Monster was wrong about humans . . . about all of them being bad.

Sure, some of them had treated me pretty rough, but the Old Lady had been kind. So had the Big Human and the Little Girl.

It seemed to me that there were good humans and bad humans, just like there were good cats and bad cats.

I began to realize I was one of the bad ones. I thought about all the times I hid under her bed when the Old Lady wanted me to come and sit on her lap.

I thought about all the times I had tricked her into giving me extra food.

I thought about when I had walked around on her tables and sat in her best chairs.

I thought about how I had slept in her nice, warm bed, while she lay on the cold kitchen floor.

I thought about how much the Little Girl had loved me and how the only thing I was thinking about when I was with her was my next meal.

There was no doubt about it.

I was a bad cat.

I wasn't even good to my fellow cats. I had pretended to be interested in the Great Cat, so the Old Cat would show me where they kept the food.

Worse, I had left Monster at the Animal Control to free the other cats. I had only thought about saving myself.

Monster was a hero. I was a jerk.

I resolved then and there to try to be a better cat. And if I ever had another human, I would treat him or her right.

There didn't seem to be much chance of that, though. No human would want me the way I looked.

Besides, now I was a wanted cat.

Chapter Fifteen. Under the FDR.
I Meet the Sarge and, Very Nearly, My Maker.

I waited a little while longer but no Monster. It was getting dark, and I was really hungry. I figured he wasn't coming and headed south, keeping in the shadows of the highway.

There were a few humans under the highway. I'd seen a few like them before, and I always steered clear of those humans.

Their clothes were all ragged and their hair was long and matted. I realized they looked a lot like me.

Some of the humans were gathered around a barrel with a fire inside it. I thought maybe they were cooking something and might give me some. Worth a shot, I figured.

As I crept closer to the fire, one of them spotted me.

"What the heck is that?"

"It's a cat of some kind," another one said.

"Never saw a cat that looked like that before. Go on cat—scat!"

He picked up a piece of broken pavement and threw it in my direction. It missed me by a mile, but I got the feeling I wouldn't be welcome around the old campfire.

But I was hungry. So instead of slinking back into the shadows, I hunkered down on the spot.

Just then another ragged human joined the group. He had some kind of stick and was using it to help him walk.

He made his way over to the barrel and warmed his hands. The other humans sort of stepped back to give him room.

"What's all the excitement?" the new human asked.

"Aw, just some kinda strange cat, man. Tryin' to grab some chow, I guess."

"Some guy we don't know?"

"Naw, Sarge," the other human said. "A real cat. Weird looking thing."

"Well, if he's looking for a handout he's out of luck around here."

The other humans sort of chuckled at that. One of them turned to the new human.

"Hey Sarge, Sammy and me are goin' over to the soup kitchen on Lex. You wanna go?"

"No, I'm going to do take-out tonight," the one they called Sarge said. "You boys be careful you don't catch religion over there."

"Not much chance of that," the other one laughed. "They wanna save my soul, they can go to it. Long as they save a hot bowl of soup for me."

The other humans drifted away. The one they called Sarge slipped off what looked like a backpack and settled down on an old lawn chair somebody had thrown away.

He looked around to make sure nobody was watching and then took something out of his backpack. It looked like a sandwich of some kind . . . "hero sandwiches," I think they're called. I'd seen Luz eat one in our kitchen.

I knew I was risking another chunk of pavement being thrown at me—and this human might have better aim— but like I told you, I was hungry.

So very carefully I approached the human called the Sarge.

It was pretty dark by then and even darker under that highway where we were, and I was using my best stealth tactics, but the human spotted me right away.

We looked at one another for a long time. Then the human broke off a little piece of his sandwich and threw it. It landed right at my feet.

I picked it up and darted back into the shadows. It wasn't much—mainly just bread—but I woofed it down fast.

I was still hungry. So I tried my move again. This time I got a piece with a little meat in it. It was delicious.

I tried a third time. But it wasn't a charm.

"Sorry cat. All gone."

I slunk back into the shadows and just lay there watching the human. He reached in his pocket and took out a small bottle, put it up to his lips and took a long drink of whatever was in it.

He sat there for a long time taking occasional pulls on his bottle. Finally, he got up. He seemed to be having a little trouble walking and his stick wasn't helping much.

I didn't want to lose this human, the one who'd shared his food with me. So I followed him at a distance.

He stopped once. I guessed he had to do one of the things I do when I use a litter box. Although it had been a long time since I'd actually had a litter box to use.

I followed him to a pile of boxes leaning against one of the columns that supported the bridge. He pushed some of the boxes aside. I could see a large cardboard box—big enough for a human to get inside. It had a piece of clear plastic taped to one side like a window.

I would have killed to have a box like that.

He looked inside it and poked about with his stick. Once he was satisfied it was empty, he reached into his backpack and took out a ragged blanket.

Just as he was about to crawl inside his box, he turned and looked at me.

"Cat, I can't even take care of myself. I sure can't take care of you."

With that, he disappeared inside the box.

I just sat there for a while . . . amazed that he could spot me in the dark. "He must have eyes like us," I thought.

I found one of the boxes the human had tossed aside and crawled into it. It was open on one end, so I could look out every once in a while and make sure the human was still there.

I didn't sleep all that well that night. I guess it was the traffic overhead keeping me awake. But maybe I was still feeling bad about leaving Monster. I was excited about finding the human they called Sarge. And I was still a little hungry.

I was awake when I saw the Sarge crawl out of his box. I crawled out of mine, too.

For a long time, we just sat there and looked at each other. I was beginning to worry that the Sarge didn't remember me.

Finally, he said, "Cat, I thought I told you to get lost. Now, beat it."

With that, he pulled himself up, stuffed his blanket in the backpack and headed toward the street. I followed him at a distance—trying to make sure he didn't see me.

His first stop was a gas station. I guess he knew the attendant, because he tossed the Sarge a key. He disappeared into a little room at the side of the station.

The Sarge came out a few minutes later, and I could

tell he'd washed up a little . . . about as much washing as
you could do at a gas station, I guess.

In the daylight, I could see a little bit more of the
Sarge. He was tall and had a long beard. His hair was tied
in back.

Last night, I had thought he was fat like I used to
be. But as he buttoned up his green overcoat, I could see
it was all the clothes he was wearing under it: a jacket, a
sweatshirt and who knows what else.

The Sarge pulled up the hood of his sweatshirt and
headed away from the river toward a street with a good bit
of traffic on it. At each corner, he'd stop and look in the
trash can. If there were soda cans or bottles inside, he'd
take them.

I couldn't imagine what possible use they could be.

I followed the Sarge for a little while longer. I was
beginning to consider going to look for something to eat,
but I didn't want to let him out of my sight.

Abruptly, he stopped and looked right at me.

"Look cat . . . don't follow me . . . you understand? I got
no need for a cat. Now scat!"

I don't know if you know this or not, but "scat" is one
of the worst things you can say to a cat. I was really hurt
that the Sarge would say that to me.

I was even more hurt when he picked up an old apple
core out of the trash can and threw it at me. It missed my
head by inches.

"Scat, I told you! Scat!"

I can take a hint, so I left the human called Sarge and
slunk back in the opposite direction.

I didn't know this part of town at all, but I was sure I

could make my way back to that place under the highway. Cats have an excellent sense of direction.

I tried a few garbage cans along the way, but the pickings were pretty slim. The hard, dry crust of a pizza was the best I could do.

I was still hungry when I got back to the under-the-highway place. I walked over to where the Sarge's box was hidden. Sure, he'd said "scat" and some other awful things . . . but maybe he'd change his mind.

Since he wasn't using his box just then, I figured I'd crawl in for a nap. I was still pretty hungry and thought maybe a nap would take my mind off my stomach.

It worked for a while—better than I thought it would, I guess, because when I woke up it was dark. Of course, it was always kind of dark under the highway, but I could tell it was almost nighttime.

I was so hungry I couldn't stand it any longer. I had to find something to eat. I headed back up the hill toward the streets that might have food places. I guess I was so busy looking for one, I didn't see the three humans on the corner.

"Hey look! That's that cat, man! The one who made me blind in my eye!"

Too late, I recognized them. The three humans who'd tried to hurt me.

"Aw, you crazy, man. That's not the cat . . . this look like some kinda alligator or something."

"I'd know that cat anywhere. Help me catch him."

The three humans started toward me, and I turned to run. But there was no place to run. They had me cornered.

The one who'd held me started taking off his jacket.

"Here kitty, kitty! I won't hurt you."

Just then the one on my left grabbed for my tail. He missed, but the human with the jacket didn't.

He threw it over me and picked it up with me inside.

"Got you now, you devil cat!"

He was holding me tight in the jacket. He pushed it down so my head was outside. I didn't like what I saw.

The human had a knife.

"Now, I'm gonna do to you what you did to me! An eye for an eye!"

He brought the shiny knife blade close to my right eye. I closed my eyes and wriggled as much as I could. I wasn't going to make it easy for him.

"Hah, you don't think I'll cut you? I'll show you, cat."

I was squirming and yowling like I never did before. But I knew it was no use. Pretty soon I'd feel that knife blade in my eye.

But then I heard a voice. It was a calm voice, but it was the kind you'd pay attention to, if you knew what was good for you.

"Whatever you do to that cat, I'm going to do to you."

I felt the human's grip loosen a little but not so much as that I could get free.

I could turn my head, though.

It was the Sarge.

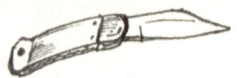

"Listen bum! You mind your own business. Me and this cat's got history together," the bad human said.

"And you'll be history if you don't drop that cat right now."

"I'm not gonna take that from no bum," the human said and dropped me like a sack of potatoes. I hit the sidewalk on my feet and took off running.

When I figured it was safe, I turned to look. The Sarge was standing there under the streetlight facing the three humans.

Actually, it was just one human—the one with the

knife. The others had pulled back a little, as if they weren't sure how this was going to end.

"You disrespected me for the last time . . . you homeless . . . bum!" Now he was standing just a foot or two from the Sarge.

The Sarge turned as if he was about to walk away. Suddenly, his walking stick came up from the sidewalk and against the human's hand. The knife he'd been holding flew up in the air.

Then the Sarge brought the stick down and caught the human on the side of his head. He went down like a load of bricks had fallen on him.

"Any of you other punks like to play with knives?" the Sarge asked the other two.

They didn't answer. They just turned and ran away.

The Sarge picked up the human's knife and slid it under the rope tied around his waist. He leaned over and felt the human's wrist. Then he looked over to me.

"Cat, you owe me one."

He started walking toward the river. He stopped and looked back at me.

"Well, come on," he said. "Don't you want something to eat?"

I followed the Sarge back to his box. He reached into his backpack and pulled out one of those long sandwiches. He broke it in half and held out half to me. It was the best food I'd eaten in a long, long time.

The Sarge drank from his the bottle . . . stretched and . . . after checking it out . . . crawled inside the box.

In a couple of minutes, I could hear him making a noise like a cat's purr—only deeper. The Old Lady had made a noise like that sometimes when she slept. It's called "snoring."

I looked around for a box of my own. I found the one

from last night. But even inside the box it was cold, really cold.

Cautiously, I approached the Sarge's box. He was still making that purring sound, so I crept in and curled up on his legs. He shifted a little and jostled me, but I didn't mind. Pretty soon, I started to purr, too.

The Sarge woke me up a few times during the night. He'd talk, and once in a while he'd yell in his sleep. Things like, "Incoming!" . . . "Watch it . . . watch it!" . . . and, "Medic!"

But I knew he wasn't yelling at me, so I went back to sleep.

Next thing I knew, it was morning. The Sarge woke me up when he moved his legs. We both climbed out of our box.

"Hope I didn't give you any new fleas," he said. "C'mon, let's go get breakfast."

I followed him out on the sidewalk. It had snowed heavily last night, and the sidewalk hadn't been shoveled. I was having a tough time walking.

After we'd stopped at a couple of trash cans, the Sarge noticed it. He took off the backpack, kneeled down, took out a blanket from his pack, picked me up and put me in it.

It was a good thing I'd lost a lot of weight, I guess. Otherwise, he'd never have been able to get me in that backpack. Even now it was a tight squeeze, because my hair was so stiff. He worked it so my head could stick out the top. Then he put the backpack back in place, tied the blanket around his waist, and we were off.

Some humans who were out early saw us and smiled. They seemed to like the idea of a human with a cat on his back.

One of those pushcart humans gave the Sarge a cup of coffee and a piece of bread of some kind. He gave half the bread to me.

We were making our way downtown, when a young female human stopped us. She was kind of pretty.

"Excuse me, could I take a picture of you and your cat?"

"Sorry ma'am," the Sarge said. "We'd just as soon you didn't."

"Well, could I ask you a couple of questions, then?" She then proceeded to ask the Sarge a whole bunch of questions—how long had he been homeless? . . . Had he been in the military? . . . Where did he get me?

The Sarge was very polite to her, but he didn't answer a single question. Finally he said, "I'm sorry, ma'am. But if you'll excuse me, we've got to get back to work."

She just nodded and we walked past her.

The Sarge couldn't see, but I could. She took our picture . . . a lot of them, in fact—me in the knapsack and the Sarge poking through a trash can.

Chapter Sixteen. First Avenue.
The Sarge Gets Mad and We Get Famous.

Life with the Sarge was pretty much the same every day. We'd go out looking for cans to sell, and in the evening the Sarge and some of the other humans would sit around the oil drum with the fire in it. I'd sit next to the Sarge, and he'd share his food with me. Then we'd go to our box.

I got to know some of the other humans living under the highway. They were nice enough to me, although they never seemed to have any food to share.

All of them seemed to respect the Sarge. Maybe they were a little afraid of him. He was bigger than the rest, and although he needed a stick to help him walk, he seemed very strong.

One day when we were out looking for cans, we passed another human wearing a coat like the one the Sarge wore.

"Can you help a fellow vet?" the human asked the Sarge.

The Sarge looked at the human and at the coat he was wearing. Then he asked him, "82nd?"

The human said, "Yeah 82nd. You?"

"Ranger," the Sarge said. "Second Gulf?"

"Yeah. Got shot up pretty bad, man."

"You guys were up near Tabriz, right?"

"Yeah . . . yeah . . . Tabriz . . . tough going up there, man."

The Sarge looked at him hard, "Maybe that's because you were in the wrong country. Tabriz is in Iran. Best I can remember, the war was in Iraq."

"Hey man . . . cut me some slack. I'm just trying to get by . . . same as you."

The Sarge took his walking stick and pointed it at the other human's face. "If I ever see you again wearing any part of a uniform you've got no right to, I'll put this stick right down your throat. Now, get off my street."

I'd never seen the Sarge so angry, and I guess the other human hadn't either. He took off right away.

The Sarge didn't say anything else for a long time.

Next day, he and I were on our regular route, when a human ran out of one of the stores waving a newspaper.

"Hey, you're the guy, right? The homeless guy with the cat?"

The Sarge just looked at him.

"See, it's right here in the paper. Your picture. You and your cat."

The Sarge took the paper the man handed him and looked at it. Then he crumpled it up and dropped it in the bag where he put the cans.

"Er . . . you can keep that one if you want to," the man said.

The Sarge didn't say anything. He just walked away.

I'd been in the backpack the whole time, of course, and I couldn't see the paper. I didn't see it until later when we passed by a newsstand.

There was this big color photo of the Sarge and me on the front page. I was in the backpack, and he was looking through the trash for cans. Our lives were different after that. For one thing, humans were nicer to us. One place would bag up all their soda cans and give them to the Sarge when we passed by.

Other places would give him food for us. And some humans would try to give him a buck or two. The Sarge wouldn't take their money, until one day a human said, "It's for the cat." After that, he took it and used it to buy me cat food.

Yeah, things were definitely better for the Sarge and me. The other humans under the highway started treating us like celebrities. Funny thing, though, none of it seemed to make much difference to the Sarge.

Chapter Seventeen. Under the FDR.
I Do Something Heroic and Get Shot For It.

We were sitting around the old oil drum one night—
the Sarge and me and a couple of other humans—when all
of a sudden the Sarge tensed up like he heard something.
My hearing is really good, but I couldn't hear anything but
the traffic on the highway overhead.

"We got visitors," the Sarge said.

Sure enough, two humans were picking their way
through the junk. One of them was a big guy with a shiny
bald head and a camera; the other was the female who'd
taken our picture. She had a flashlight.

"Hi," she said. "Could we talk? Oh, this is John, one
of our real photographers. I'm just an amateur, but that
shot of you and your cat came out real well, don't you
think?"

The Sarge just stared at the two of them.

"I guess I should introduce myself, too. I'm Judy Levine

of the *Daily News*. But I guess you already know who I work for."

"This human female sure talks a lot," I was thinking.

"It isn't safe for you two to be here," the Sarge said. "You should go back to your newspaper and leave us alone."

"Don't worry," the big human said. "We've been in some tight spots before. And we're used to not being welcome."

"I don't mean to be rude, but I would really appreciate it if you wouldn't bother us anymore," the Sarge said.

"Oh, but our readers are really interested in you and your cat," the female said. "All we want is just to find out a little bit about you two."

"Look man," the big human said, "we got a job to do. Give us a few minutes and we'll be out of your hair."

"I'm sorry . . ." the Sarge stopped and held up his hand as if he heard something else.

"Quick get behind that column, and don't show yourselves until I say it's OK." He picked me up and handed me to the female. "Here, take my cat."

We got behind the column all right, but the two humans couldn't help themselves—they had to peek around the corner of the column to see what was going on. Of course, so did I.

What we saw was three humans with flashlights. Two of them were also carrying baseball bats. One also had a can that seemed to be full of some kind of funny-smelling liquid. And the third human—he had a gun.

I knew all about guns, thanks to the Old Lady. She loved opera and museums and all, but she was crazy about cop shows on TV. I couldn't help but pick up a thing or two just from being in the room.

This gun was a pistol. I saw the gun before I saw the human holding it.

It was the one who had tried to hurt me with the knife.

"There's the bum!" the human yelled, "the one who broke my hand."

"If your hand is broken, that's going to affect your aim," the Sarge said quietly.

"You . . . you shut up! You disrespected me for the last time. I'm gonna blow you away, and then we're gonna burn out the rest of you homeless bums."

He was pointing the gun directly at the Sarge. The bad human's hand was shaking.

"If you plan to hit anybody with that peashooter, you'd better get in closer," the Sarge said.

"Stop telling me stuff!" he shouted. "You think I don't know how to use this thing? You think I never shot anybody before?"

"That's exactly what I think," the Sarge said. "Otherwise, you wouldn't have the safety on."

"Hah! I'm not falling for that! I checked it before I came in here. It's loaded . . . it's cocked . . . safety's off . . . and you are gonna die."

"So you're going to shoot me in front of witnesses, huh?"

"You mean the broad and the black guy hiding behind that post? You got them to thank for helping us find you. They were asking around about a homeless guy and a cat. All we had to do is follow them."

The bad human wiped his nose with his sleeve and continued talking, holding the pistol on the Sarge with his other hand.

"First, I'm gonna take care of you . . . then I'll whack them and put the gun in your hand. It'll look like some crazy homeless guy shot two people and then offed himself."

"Then," he said, "I'm gonna find that cat."

I have to tell you my first impulse was to run for it. But something kept me from doing that.

It wasn't that stuff about being a better cat and all. To tell the truth, I wasn't thinking about myself. I was thinking about the Sarge.

I couldn't let this guy shoot him. I knew I was a coward, but I also knew I had to do something. Or at least try.

"Your beef is with me," the Sarge was telling the human. "Let the others go and we'll settle this—just you and me."

"You—shut up!" the bad human screamed. With that he kicked the Sarge's stick, and the Sarge went down.

The Sarge was on the ground with his stick maybe a foot away. And the human pointing the gun at his head.

"You see how it feels, bum? Now you gonna feel how it feels to die!"

This was it. I had to make my move. Now.

My plan—if you could call it a plan—was to come out in the open, so the human would see me. I figured he'd start chasing me, and the Sarge and the others could escape. As soon as the human saw me, I'd run to the right as fast as I could.

I squirmed out of the female's arms and ran out from behind the column. I realized right away my plan wouldn't work. There was so much junk on the ground the human couldn't see me.

There was only one way I could get the bad human's attention. And that was to run straight toward him.

Straight toward him and his gun.

I was maybe halfway to him when I realized it wasn't such a good plan, either. I got the human's attention, all right. Enough for him to point his pistol toward me—and fire.

Just then there was a brilliant flash of light, and something struck the bad human in the head. He staggered for a second or two and then went down.

For a guy with a bad leg, the Sarge could move really fast. He had managed to grab his stick and bring it up hard to one side of the human's head and then grab the gun as the bad guy went down.

The other two humans—the ones with the bats and cans—ran. They didn't want any part of a homeless guy with a gun.

The big human and the female came running out from behind the column.

"Did you get that?" the female was screaming at the big human. "Did you get the shot?"

"I think so. Yeah, I did. Look at this."

They were looking at the back of his camera. Meanwhile, the Sarge had his foot—the one with the good leg—on the human's head.

The other homeless people, who had run when the gang showed up, drifted back. I heard one of them call out—

"Hey Sarge . . . I think your cat's been shot."

Chapter Eighteen. West 72nd Street.
I Get a Lion Cut and Learn of My Inheritance.

Shot? I hadn't realized it until then. Yeah, come to think of it my back did feel like it was on fire, and my hair was getting all wet. I was kind of dizzy, so I lay down.

"Jerry—get some rags and tie this guy up. Tom—bring that flashlight over here, will you."

The Sarge rushed over to me and looked at my back while the human Tom held the flashlight.

"Can't tell how bad it is with all this hair. But he's losing blood. A lot of blood."

"C'mon Sarge," one of the other homeless humans was saying. "We gotta get outta here before the cops come."

"You guys take off. I can't leave him."

I was kind of drifting in and out, so I couldn't really tell what was going on. The female was clicking away at her phone . . . the big human was holding the gun on the one on the ground . . . and I could hear a siren.

"Put your hands in the air!" the policeman shouted. "All of you."

Everybody did except the Sarge. He stood up, but his hands were full of me.

"What's going on here?" another policeman wanted to know.

The female took it on herself to answer. She told the policemen that she was a reporter for the *Daily News* and had a press pass in her pocket, and if they would let her put her hands down she would show them.

Then she explained how the bad human and his gang had threatened the people living here and had pulled a gun on this man—the Sarge she meant—and how the cat had tried to jump the bad guy and now he was shot and needed medical attention, and she knew that the officer had a first-aid kit in his car and would he please get it before the cat bled to death?

"A cat jumped the gunman." the policeman said. "You gotta be kidding."

"It's true," she said, "and if you don't want to see a headline in tomorrow's paper that says, COPS DENY AID TO HERO CAT, you'll get that first-aid kit."

One of the officers ran away and came back with the kit. He knelt over me and put some stingy stuff on my wound. Then he wrapped some kind of towel around me.

"That'll stop the bleeding for a while. But this cat needs a real doc."

"I don't think there is any such thing as a twenty-four-hour veterinarian," the Sarge said.

"Are you kidding?" It was the female. "This is New York City! I just called a vet I know over on the West Side. Woke him up and told him to be ready for us."

Meanwhile, the other policeman had put the cuffs on the human who'd shot me. By that time, another squad car with two more policemen had arrived.

"Hey! Guess who this guy is, Pete. It's the punk who pulled all those bodega jobs," one of the cops yelled.

"OK, we'll take him in." He turned to the Sarge.

"I'm going to need you to come down to the station for a statement."

"I'm not going anywhere until my cat is taken care of," the Sarge said.

"Uh . . . OK, you can come in tomorrow."

"And you can take us to the vet," the female said to the policeman. Can't get there any faster than in a cop car."

"Lady, I can't do that . . . we got procedures we got to follow."

"OK how about this—COP DENIES MERCY RIDE FOR DYING HERO CAT—and I'll make sure your name is spelled right, Officer Kowalski."

"OK, you win. Get in the car."

I don't remember much about the ride . . . the female . . . the Sarge and me crowded in the back of a patrol car. I do remember the siren wailing and me feeling very sick.

Some people think cats have nine lives. If that were true, I figured I'd already used up about eight of mine.

And I wasn't sure if this one was going to last until we got to the West Side.

The Sarge and the female took me inside the Vet's place. It wasn't my regular Vet, but at that point I didn't feel like arguing. The Vet looked as if he'd just been rousted out of bed, but he woke up pretty quickly when he saw me.

"My cat's been shot," the Sarge was telling him. "I don't have any money, but if you can help him, I'll get you whatever it takes."

They took me into another room, and the Vet
examined my back, where I'd been shot. He shook his
head.

"I can't tell much with all this matted hair. We'll have
to shave him, so I can get at the wound. He's lost a lot of
blood. That I can tell."

The Vet gave me a shot that didn't hurt nearly as much
as the one I'd gotten from the human's gun. He started an
IV drip . . . I knew about those already.

Pretty soon I was out cold. When I woke up, I had a
big bandage on my back. And most of my hair was gone. I
thought that was weird but not for long. I was asleep again
before I could think any more about it.

When I woke again, I was in a cage—much nicer than
the one at the Control place. The Sarge was standing in
front of the cage looking at me through the wire.

"Well Cat, I guess you taking a bullet for me makes us
even. Now you just hurry and get well, so we can get back
to work."

"He's a very lucky cat," I heard the Vet telling the
Sarge. "Another half inch and the bullet would have gone
into his spine. But it looks like all that hard, matted hair
helped deflect it."

So now I had what they were calling a "lion cut." I got
a glimpse of my reflection in a shiny steel cabinet. All of my
hair except for my head, legs, and tail was gone. I guess I
was supposed to look like a lion. I looked like a freak.

I fell asleep again, and when I woke up I could hear the
Sarge and the Vet talking.

"I couldn't help but notice the Ranger tabs on your
jacket," the Vet was saying to the Sarge. "Were you in
Iraq?"

"Iraq . . . Kuwait . . . Afghanistan . . . probably some
other places I can't remember," the Sarge replied.

"Gulf Two?" the Vet asked.

"Both," the Sarge said. "I was going to go for twenty . . . career, right? But my leg got kind of messed up on my last tour, and I was mustered out."

"I saw a little bit of the Mid East myself on Uncle Sam's dime," the Vet said.

"Were you a doc?" Sarge asked.

"No, I was a newly-minted infantry second lieutenant when I went over. Major by the time I got back from my last tour."

"So how did you get into this?" the Sarge asked.

"Figured I'd seen enough people trying to kill each other. So when I got out I went to veterinary school. Never expected to work on a cat with a gunshot wound, though."

The Vet paused for a minute.

"I don't mean to pry, but are you getting any kind of benefits now?"

"If you mean can I pay for my cat, I told you I'd get you the money," I heard the Sarge say.

"Listen, I'm not worried about that. I got enough free advertising from being the Vet who 'saved the Hero Cat.' Everybody and his brother wants to bring their pets here now."

"Well," the Sarge said, "I signed over most of my benefits to my wife . . . ex-wife, I mean. As for the rest, I guess the VA has given up trying to find me."

"Maybe I can help," the Vet said. "There are a couple of guys in Washington who owe me big-time. Oh, that reminds me, I was so busy I forgot to check your cat for a chip."

"A chip?"

"Yeah, some owners have a microchip implanted in their animals. It can identify them if they get lost."

"Will it hurt him? He's been through a lot, you know."

"No, I just run this wand over his body, and if there's a

chip the machine will read it."

The Vet paused again.

"Of course, if you'd rather not, I won't. You see, if there is a chip, I'll have to notify the owners."

It was the Sarge's turn to go quiet then. "No, go ahead and check, Doc. If he's got an owner, I'm sure he'd be better off with them than me."

The Vet called in his assistant, a young male human. They got me out of the cage and waved what appeared to be a TV remote all over my body. There was a beep, and some numbers came up on a screen.

The Vet told his assistant to call the company that put the chip in, and when he came back he was really excited.

"Holy cow!" the young human shouted. "This is the Van Den Pelt cat!"

"What's a Van Den Pelt cat?" the Sarge wanted to know.

"We get these bulletins from time to time for lost or strayed pets. This one I remembered. You see, the owner's estate is offering a large reward."

"I have to report this, you know," the Vet said to the Sarge. He didn't sound happy about it.

"Sure, Doc. Do what you have to do. Guess now would be a good time for me to move on, anyway."

"No, at least stick around until this thing is resolved. There's a reward, you know."

"I don't want their money," the Sarge said. "Don't need it."

"It may take a while for us to get in touch with the lawyers handling this. In the meantime, your cat could use your company. It'll help him get well, believe me."

So I was the Van Den Pelt cat, huh? I guess they called me that because that was the Old Lady's name.

But it wasn't any more my real name than Boo was.

Chapter Nineteen. 60 Centre Street.
I Have My Day in Court.

I dozed off again and when I woke up, there was the Sarge looking in through the grille.

I almost didn't recognize him. His hair had been cut and so had his beard. In the place of his old ragged clothes, he was wearing a neat, white uniform.

"Looks like I got a job, Cat. They're going to let me help out around here for a while. So I can keep an eye on you."

He winked at me. I'd never seen the Sarge wink before. I didn't know what to think.

It's funny. People will say anything to each other in front of a cat. I guess they don't think we know what they're saying.

It turns out the Sarge and the Vet had more in common than just being in Iraq at the same time. They both had some kind of problem, and the Vet was trying to

talk the Sarge into going to a meeting with him. He said
he'd think about it.

I didn't understand what any of that meant. And I had
other things to worry about. I was afraid this lawyer who
was coming would take me away from the Sarge.

I guess it was the next day when he showed up. I
recognized him right away. I had seen him at the Old
Lady's place many times. He was Barlow, her lawyer.
Barlow was wearing a black suit and a black tie. He had a
long beak of a nose and very little hair. He looked like one
of the vultures I'd seen on the Old Lady's nature programs.

He didn't recognize me, of course. He'd never paid that
much attention to me anyway, and besides, now I looked
a lot different. I wasn't fat anymore. And I didn't have my
nice, long hair.

They ran the chip thing again, and Barlow looked at
the screen and at a strip of paper a machine printed out.
He asked if he could meet the Sarge.

Barlow and the Sarge talked for a while. Then Barlow
spoke to the Vet alone. There was a stupid dog barking, so
I couldn't hear everything, but the lawyer said something
about a judge having to decide.

This was getting more complicated by the moment. I
had no idea just how complicated it would get—

For the next few weeks, things were pretty normal.
I was much better, so they let me out of that cage and I
moved in with the Sarge, in a little room over the Vet's
place.

The Sarge worked at the Vet's, sweeping up and taking
care of the animals. I could tell he liked doing it. He and
the Vet would go to one of those meetings every Monday
night.

That female reporter person dropped by almost every
day. She said she was checking up on me, but I think she
really came to see the Sarge.

He looked a lot different now. Really sharp—for a human.

Me, I still had that stupid lion cut. I looked ridiculous.

Most of the time, the Sarge would bring me downstairs with him while he worked. I had to stay in my portable cage and away from the other cats, so I wouldn't catch anything from those that came in sick.

The Sarge and the Vet spent a lot of time talking to each other. They kept their voices low, but I could hear every word.

They mostly talked about "the hearing," when my future would be decided. The Vet wanted to hire a lawyer, but the Sarge said he couldn't afford one.

The next day the female reporter showed up with another human. He had snow-white hair and spots on his hands. His name was Farnsworth, and he was the oldest human I'd ever seen. And he was going to be my lawyer. I heard them say that Farnsworth was going to be representing the Sarge for free. When the Sarge said he couldn't let Mr. Farnsworth do that, the lawyer cut him off.

"Sergeant, I'm a veteran, too. Korea. And we vets have to stick together. Besides, without me you'll lose the cat."

I learned later that Farnsworth had been one of the top lawyers in New York. And one of the most expensive.

The first thing Farnsworth did was to get the Sarge to agree to an interview with the female reporter. There had already been a lot of stuff about us in the papers and on TV. But the lawyer said he wanted to make sure people knew what kind of human the Sarge was.

It turned out that the female reporter was a really big deal at the *Daily News*. It was an important newspaper, but I'd never heard of it until we met her. The Old Lady only read *The Times*.

The next thing Farnsworth did was take the Sarge with him to buy a suit for the hearing. The Sarge kept telling him that he couldn't afford a suit, but Farnsworth said it was a gift from a couple of old clients of his, the Brooks Brothers.

The Sarge looked really good in that suit the morning we left for the courthouse. I hadn't realized I would be going. But Farnsworth said it was important that I be there. I happened to agree with him, so I got into the carrier without complaining.

The hearing was in a big building downtown with huge columns and a lot of steps. People were already lined up on the steps waiting for us.

Some of them were carrying signs. They said things like, "Let the Vet Keep his Cat" and "Hero Cat to Hero Vet." At least, that's what somebody told me they said.

I don't read human that well.

I was confused until I heard somebody say they were calling the Sarge "the vet," even though he wasn't a veterinarian. It was because he had been in the Army and that made him a veteran or vet for short.

People cheered when they saw us. Others were taking pictures of us like crazy. There were TV crews with lights and cameras.

And me looking like a plucked chicken with that stupid lion cut.

We went up the steps and into a huge, marble lobby . . . then up more stairs, until we got to a big room with lots of seats. There was a huge desk at the end of the room with flags on both sides of it.

Farnsworth, the Sarge and I went down to the front of the room and were given seats at a large table. The Sarge put my carrier on the floor next to his chair. But Farnsworth whispered in his ear, and he put me and the carrier up on the table. I could see everything.

One of the first things I saw was old Barlow. He was sitting at a table directly across from us. He took a quick look in my direction and started sneezing. It wasn't long before his beak of a nose was all red. He kept dabbing at it with a handkerchief. In between sneezes, that is.

I saw Barlow write something on a piece of paper and give it to one of his assistants. The assistant rushed out of the courtroom.

I noticed that Farnsworth was watching all this, too.

One of the humans shouted for everybody to rise, and all the other humans did. I was already standing in my carrier.

A female human dressed in a black robe came in and sat down behind the desk. Then all the other humans sat down. I sat down, too.

I knew that the female in the black robe was called "a judge." I knew that from being in the room while the Old Lady watched a TV show about a judge called Judy. I guess some of it stuck.

"Ordinarily, I'd hold a hearing like this in my chambers," the judge said, "but because of the extraordinary interest in this matter, I've decided to hold it in open court.

"I hope I don't regret that decision."

There was a murmur from the humans a little like laughter, and the judge banged her gavel. I remembered that it was called "a gavel" from TV, too.

"There will be no photographs allowed and no cameras of any kind in my courtroom. Do I make myself clear?"

There was no murmur this time. She went on speaking.

"This hearing is to decide the future of a certain cat—which has been left a considerable inheritance by his late owner, a Mrs. Meriwether Van Den Pelt of this city." She continued, "The court will decide if this cat is to remain with a Mr. Stephen Cole or to be placed in the custody of Mrs. Van Den Pelt's attorney, Mr. Hubert Barlow.

"It is the court's understanding that the inheritance bequeathed to this cat will be placed in trust and utilized solely for the maintenance of the cat. But that the party awarded custody of this cat will have discretionary usage of these funds.

"Does everybody understand all that?" the judge asked. I don't think she really expected an answer.

She called on Barlow first, and he stood up facing the judge.

"Your Honor, I must apologize for taking up the court's valuable time with what should be a simple matter. We are asking that this cat, whose name by the way is Boo, be cared for in accordance with Mrs. Van Den Pelt's wishes—that he be taken care of for the rest of his natural life . . . surrounded by those who love him."

Old Barlow was really on a roll now. "My client—the late Mrs. Van Den Pelt—dearly loved Boo, and she has generously made provisions for his care in her will. I refer the court to article two, section one—"

"I've read the will, Mr. Barlow. You don't have to read it again," the judge said.

Barlow continued, "In accordance with Mrs. Van Den Pelt's wishes and subject to approval by this court, I have made arrangements for Boo to remain in the apartment he shared with his late owner and to be cared for by two persons who know and love him—her maid Mrs. Luz Gutierrez and her cook Miss Rose Wilson."

There they were, the two people who had hated me all the time I lived with the Old Lady. It would be bad enough to be separated from the Sarge. But life with those two would be unbearable.

Luz was all dressed up and was looking around the courtroom as if she were the star of the show. Rose just sat there looking like she wanted to be someplace else.

Then Barlow turned to the judge and said, "Your Honor, I would now like to call Mrs. Gutierrez to the stand."

You could tell Luz was pleased to be the center of attention. She made the most of her walk up to the chair next to the judge. Luz put her hand on the book and repeated the words the bailiff had said.

Old Barlow asked Luz a few questions, like how long had she worked for the Old Lady, and then he got around to the important stuff.

"Mrs. Gutierrez, could you please tell about the morning you found Mrs. Van Den Pelt lying on the kitchen floor?"

"Oh yes. It was a very sad day for everyone. We loved the Old . . . the Señora."

"And how did you feel about Boo, her cat?"

"Oh, I loved that cat like he was my own. He was the nicest, sweetest thing you could imagine."

I was stunned! There was old Luz, who always hated me, saying all those things. How could she lie like that?

Barlow said he had no further questions and that Luz could step down. He turned to the judge and said, "And in addition to the loving care that will be provided by Mrs. Gutierrez and Mrs. Wilson, I personally will make regular visits accompanied by one of the city's leading veterinarians to assure Boo's wellbeing."

With that, Barlow sat down. He looked rather pleased with himself. His nose had stopped running, but my heart was pounding.

What if the judge believed him? Or Luz? I'd be

snatched away from the Sarge and held prisoner by
people who hated me.

Things weren't looking good for me. Not good at all.

Chapter Twenty. 60 Centre Street.
Barlow Orders Out.

Farnsworth may have been the oldest human in the courtroom. But when it was his turn to speak, his voice was loud and clear.

"Your Honor, I 'd like to call Sergeant Ronald Malloy to the stand."

A policeman came up and sat down next to the judge. I didn't have any idea who he was until the bailiff swore him in. I recognized his voice. Cats are very good at that kind of thing.

Farnsworth asked him if he was the officer in charge when Mrs. Van Den Pelt's body had been discovered. The policeman said that he was. Then he asked him if he recalled any comment Mrs. Gutierrez might have made that morning.

The policeman looked at his little notebook.

"She said, 'He's fat and lazy, and he sheds all over the

place.' Then she said, 'Besides, black cats like him are bad luck.'"

"Thank you, Sergeant Malloy," Farnsworth said. "Just one more question—after Boo escaped, was any effort made to try and find him?"

"We looked around the hall, but we had another call, so we couldn't spend any more time there. We notified Animal Control before we left."

"And did Mrs. Gutierrez seem concerned about Boo at that point?"

"Objection!" Barlow shouted. "That calls for a conclusion from the witness."

"Sustained," the judge said.

"No further questions, Your Honor. Now, with the court's permission, I'd like to recall Mrs. Gutierrez to the stand."

Luz looked surprised and not nearly as pleased to be the center of attention this time. She was even less pleased when old Farnsworth started to work.

"Mrs. Gutierrez, may I ask where you've been employed since Mrs. Van Den Pelt died?"

"Uh . . . I haven't had a job, sir."

"But you would have a job, if you were hired to take care of Boo, am I right?"

"Uh . . . I guess so."

"Now, Mrs. Gutierrez, you've heard Sergeant Malloy's testimony. Do you recall saying that Boo was fat and lazy and sheds all over the place? And that cats like him are bad luck?"

"I . . . I . . . I was upset. I didn't know what I was saying."

"Mrs. Gutierrez, do you know what perjury is?" Farnsworth asked.

Luz shook her head.

"Well, it means not telling the truth under oath, and

it's a serious crime. Now, do you want to reconsider your answer as to how you felt about Boo?"

"I don't know what to say!" Luz started sobbing. I almost felt sorry for her.

"No further questions for Mrs. Gutierrez, Your Honor. But with the court's permission, I'd like to call opposing counsel to the stand."

"Uh . . . this is highly irregular," old Barlow said.

"It is irregular," the judge agreed. "Mr. Farnsworth, I assume you have a good reason for such an unusual request?"

"I do, Your Honor. If we are trying to determine which party is best qualified to take care of Boo, then I believe we should examine Mr. Barlow's qualifications."

The judge reluctantly agreed, and Barlow took the seat next to the judge. He didn't look very happy about doing it, though.

"As a fellow officer of the court, of course, there's no need for you to be sworn in," Farnsworth said to Barlow.

Old Barlow just sort of huffed at that. Farnsworth went right on with his questions.

"Mr. Barlow, am I correct in assuming that if you were awarded guardianship of Boo, you would be compensated to some degree?"

"Yes, of course. There would be certain expenses for which I would be compensated, and these would be paid from the estate."

"But isn't it true that you would have almost unlimited access to the money left to Boo? That you would have sole discretion as to how the funds are spent?"

"Well . . . there are certain provisions for such in the will . . ."

"In other words, you could spend Boo's money as if it were your own?"

"I object! This line of questioning is entirely improper,"

Barlow yelled.

The judge said, "May I remind counsel that a witness cannot object. And you are, at this point in time, a witness."

Barlow didn't like that a bit. He liked Farnsworth's next question even less.

"Mr. Barlow, I've noticed you keep blowing your nose and wiping your eyes—do you perhaps have a cold?"

"Uh no . . . allergies, actually. Although I appreciate counsel's concern, I don't see what that has to do with anything."

"And what are you allergic to?"

"Dust . . . dander . . . the usual things."

"Mr. Barlow, is it not true that you are extremely allergic to—cats?"

"Uh well . . ."

"And is it not true that you had to take prescription medication every time you called on Mrs. Van Den Pelt—because she had a cat?"

"How . . . how . . . how did you know that?" Barlow stammered.

"And yet, you would have us believe that you—someone severely allergic to cats—would be a proper guardian for one."

"That's neither here nor there. I demand to know how you knew—"

"No further questions, Your Honor," Farnsworth said.

Barlow tried to say something, but the judge pounded her gavel so loudly you couldn't hear him. Then she asked Farnsworth if he had any other witnesses to call.

"Your Honor, I'd like to have Mr. Cole sworn in as a witness."

"Bailiff, swear in Mr. Cole."

This time it was the Sarge's turn to sit in the chair, put his hand on the book, and swear to tell the truth. When all that was done, Farnsworth started with his questions.

"Sergeant Cole—I'm sorry, Mr. Cole—may I ask you how you supported yourself while you were . . . homeless?"

"Yes sir. Mostly, I'd collect cans and bottles from the trash and turn them in for the deposit."

"Did you ever beg or ask people for money?"

"No sir. After Boo showed up, sometimes people would give me money for him. I bought him food with it. But I never asked anybody for money."

"So you never squeegeed windshields or anything like that?" old Farnsworth asked with a kind of smile.

"No sir. I just couldn't do that."

"Did you ever try to get a real job?"

"Yes sir. Plenty of times. I didn't have much luck, though. People didn't think a guy with a bum leg could do much, I guess."

Farnsworth paused to let that sink in.

"Now, Sergeant . . . I mean Mr. Cole . . . would you please describe how Boo the cat came to be with you?"

"Yes sir," the Sarge replied. "He just showed up one night, cold and hungry. I gave him a piece of my sandwich."

"Did you mean to keep him with you by giving him food?"

"No sir. He looked like he was starving, so I gave him a bite."

"Did you encourage him to stay with you?"

"No sir. I tried to discourage him. But he just kept hanging around."

"Now will you describe your first encounter with the person who shot Boo."

"That individual was holding a knife on Boo and threatening to cut his eye out."

"And what did you do when you witnessed that?"

"I stopped him from doing it."

Another murmur from the audience. The judged

banged her gavel but didn't say anything.

"How did you stop him?'

"I hit him with my cane."

There was another murmur but the judge ignored it.

"And your next encounter with this . . . individual?"

"That was when he shot him . . . Boo, I mean."

"Your Honor, if it please the court, I'd like to introduce into evidence Exhibit A, a copy of the February 11 edition of the *Daily News.*"

He handed a copy of the newspaper to the judge.

"As you will see, there on the front page is a color photograph of Boo the cat attempting to defend Sergeant—I mean Mr.—Cole from the gunman."

At that point, old Barlow jumped out and shouted, "Objection! Your Honor, I fail to see how a photograph we've all seen hundreds of times has any bearing on the matter."

"Mr. Farnsworth," the judge said. "I tend to agree with counsel. Just what is your point?"

"Simply that Boo cared so much for Sergeant Cole he was willing to risk his life for him."

"That's ridiculous," Barlow shouted. "The cat could have just as easily been running away from danger."

"Running toward a man with a gun hardly seems like 'running away from danger,'" Farnsworth countered.

The judge pounded her gavel.

"If you two are making your closing arguments, you are somewhat premature," she said. "I suggest you stop this banter and get on with it."

"Just few more questions, Your Honor." Farnsworth turned to the Sarge.

"Mr. Cole . . . may I ask you why you use the cane?"

"I was wounded, sir. In Iraq. They tried to fix the leg . . . and I guess they did the best they could."

"Your Honor, I'd like to enter as Exhibit B . . . Mr.

Cole's service record. And I ask the court's permission to read some of it aloud."

"Objection!" Barlow shouted again. But the judge overruled him again. Just like Judge Judy.

Mr. Farnsworth took out his glasses and wiped them off with his handkerchief. "Your Honor, I'll just read the highlights, if I might.

"'Master Sergeant Stephen B. Cole, U.S. Army, 75th Ranger Regiment . . . served in Kuwait, Iraq, Afghanistan and Saudi Arabia and other locations classified for reasons of national security . . . selected for and attended NCO Academy . . . graduated first in his class . . . received a Bachelor of Science degree from George Washington University while on active duty . . . awarded both the Silver Star and the Bronze Star for valor . . . received the Purple Heart medal and various medals from the governments of Kuwait and Saudi Arabia . . . offered and declined two battlefield commissions . . . and . . . oh . . . one other . . . nominated for the Congressional Medal of Honor.'"

You could have heard a pin drop in that courtroom. Finally, Barlow broke the silence.

"Your Honor, Sergeant . . . I mean Mr. Cole's exemplary record of service to our country is not in question. What is in question is his ability to care for this cat."

Then it was Barlow's turn to question the Sarge.

"Mr. Cole—how exactly did you become homeless?"

"Same as most people, sir. I didn't have a place to live."

There was some laughter in the courtroom. The judge banged her gavel.

"Isn't it true that like most homeless people you have a drinking problem?" Barlow asked.

"I don't know about most homeless people, sir. But yes, I do. I go to AA meetings to try to solve it."

"So you no longer drink?"

"Not since Boo got shot."

Barlow couldn't think of any more questions, but the Sarge asked if he could speak. The judge said he could.

"Your Honor, it's no secret that I want to keep Boo with me. I think I could take care of him, and we'd be just fine . . . and we wouldn't need any of Mrs. Van Den Pelt's money."

Then the judge spoke.

"Mr. Cole, Mrs. Van Den Pelt's intent was very clear. She intended to provide for her cat after her demise. There is no provision for separating custody of the cat and the money she left.

"In other words," the judge said, "she left the money to the cat. It's his."

"Your Honor," the Sarge said. "I want what's best for Boo. And if that means he goes back to his apartment . . . well . . . I guess that's the way it has to be."

Then old Barlow stood up and asked the judge for a fifteen-minute recess. The judge looked as if she could use a break, so she agreed.

I could see Barlow telling one of his assistants to do something. I couldn't hear what they were saying because of all the talking in the courtroom, but the assistant left the courtroom in a big hurry. He was back in a few minutes and handed Barlow a small paper bag. He quickly put it in his briefcase.

Barlow then asked Rose to come and sit next to him at his table. I didn't see Luz anywhere. I guess Barlow decided she wouldn't be much help.

The bailiff called the court back in session, and the judge took her seat. Right away Barlow hopped up and asked her if he and Farnsworth could approach the bench—that was the judge's desk—and talk to her. She agreed.

Both lawyers had their backs to me, and I couldn't hear what was being said. But I could tell old Farnsworth didn't like what Barlow was saying.

The judge seemed to, though. Then she ordered the bailiff to bring my cage to the space in front of her bench. Both lawyers took their seats, and old Barlow quickly opened his briefcase.

"I'm no Solomon," the judge said. "But I think counsel's solution for the question of who gets custody of the cat is as good as any I can think of."

"Bailiff," she said, "release the cat."

A gasp went up from the crowd, and everybody stood to get a better view. The bailiff human opened the door to my cage, and I walked out.

I looked at Barlow and Rose, and I looked at the Sarge.

Then I ran across the room as fast as I could.

I sprang up on the table.

And jumped right into the Sarge's arms.

I would have gone for his lap, but I couldn't get past the edge of the table.

The crowd went wild. (I've heard people say that, and I always wanted to say it myself.) They stood up and cheered and whistled. The judge kept banging her gavel until they quieted down.

Old Barlow kept trying to get the judge's attention. She shushed the crowd with her gavel and let him speak.

"Your Honor—how do we know that this man didn't use some trick to get the cat to come to him? I demand that he be searched for hidden cat food."

Farnsworth wasn't having any of that.

"Your Honor, this man is a war hero. To suggest that he might have lured the cat with cat food in his pocket is an affront to the men and women of our armed forces!"

The Sarge stood up and said, "Your Honor, it's all right if they search me. They won't find any cat food in my pockets . . . I wouldn't mess up my only suit."

People in the courtroom laughed and applauded. The judged banged her gavel again.

Farnsworth then stood up to have his say.

"Your Honor—may I suggest that if anyone is to be searched it should be opposing counsel. I believe you'll find a tuna sandwich in his briefcase."

"Mr. Barlow, do you have a tuna sandwich in your briefcase?" the judge asked.

"Well, yes, Your Honor . . . it's my lunch."

"Am I to believe that one of New York's most prominent—and most expensive—attorneys brings his own lunch?" the judge wanted to know.

"Well . . . we try to be frugal when our client's money is at stake."

"Mr. Barlow, I have no way of proving that you brought that tuna sandwich to try to make it appear that the cat favored you," the judge said. "But I can and will find you in contempt of court for bringing food into my courtroom."

Barlow sputtered and the crowd applauded. The judge let them go on for a while then started pounding her gavel.

"By the power vested in me by the State of New York, I hereby award custody of the cat known as Boo to Sergeant—I mean Mr. Stephen A. Cole. Court is adjourned."

Chapter Twenty-One. West 72nd Street.
Monster and I Meet Again.

We were almost mobbed by people when we left the courtroom. They were cheering and shouting. It made me a little jumpy.

The female reporter, the Sarge, Farnsworth and me rode back to the Vet's in Farnsworth's big car. It was even bigger than the Old Lady's. The driver sat in front. The four of us sat in back.

The reporter couldn't wait to ask Farnsworth how he had known about Barlow's cat allergy and the sandwich in his briefcase.

"Oh, I guess he hadn't figured on Boo being in the courtroom, and he didn't bring his prescription meds. I was watching him, and as soon as he saw Boo, Barlow wrote something on a piece of paper and handed it to one of his clerks.

"When the clerk came rushing back a few minutes

later with a Duane Reed bag, I surmised he'd sent for some over-the-counter pills for his allergies."

"But how did you know he was allergic to cats?" the reporter asked.

"Well, you see, Mrs. Van Den Pelt's banker and I were fraternity brothers at Yale. I called him when I took on Boo's case, and he said it was funny that Barlow would be involved.

"When I asked him why, he told me that he knew from his visits with him to Mrs. Van Den Pelt's that Barlow had a severe allergy—to cats."

All the humans laughed at that. I didn't think it was that funny.

"But how did you know about the tuna fish in the briefcase?" she asked.

"That one was easy," Farnsworth said. "When Luz came apart on the stand, Barlow knew he was in trouble. So he sent his clerk out again, and this time he came back with a brown bag, which Barlow proceeded to stuff into his briefcase.

"It looked like the same kind of bag my deli uses for takeout, and I thought that was a little unusual that he'd be putting a bag of food in his briefcase," Farnsworth continued. "So I figured Barlow had something up his sleeve. Turns out it was a tuna sandwich."

The humans laughed again, this time even harder. But it just reminded me I hadn't had lunch.

"One last question," the reporter said. "What made you so sure Boo wouldn't go for the sandwich?"

"Oh, a good lawyer knows his client. I believed Boo's feelings for Sergeant Cole would trump any hunger pangs. And I was right."

They didn't talk anymore until we got back to the Vet's.

For the next few weeks, the phone didn't stop ringing.

Reporters wanted to interview the Sarge. Photographers wanted to take our pictures. TV crews camped outside our place. Letterman and Leno wanted me and the Sarge to appear on their shows.

The Sarge turned them all down. After a while, people left us pretty much alone.

We, the Sarge and I, that is, moved to a place of our own. It wasn't Park Avenue, but it was ours and it was nice. There were lots of windows so I could take naps in the sunlight and big radiators that pumped out plenty of heat.

Old Farnsworth was still in the picture. He arranged for the Sarge to see one of New York's top surgeons to see if his leg could be fixed. The surgeon was sure it could be, but the Sarge said it would have to wait for a while.

The Sarge had a job.

Some people from the Mayor's Office had come around and told the Sarge they wanted him to head up an agency that helped the homeless. They figured nobody could do more for the homeless than somebody who'd been one.

So the Sarge got his picture taken again—this time with the mayor shaking his hand. They wanted me to be in the photo, but I figured this was the Sarge's show. So I hid under a table.

The mayor gave the Sarge a big office down at City Hall, but he didn't spend much time there. Mostly, he was out talking to the homeless humans and trying to help them.

Sometimes I went with him. The homeless humans seemed to like seeing us together, and they'd come up and talk to us. I guess they figured a guy and a cat couldn't do them much harm.

Weekends, he'd help the Vet in his clinic. Usually, I'd go with him there, too.

One of those times when the Sarge and I were at the Vet's, I heard a familiar voice. I looked and sure enough it was—Monster! What was really surprising was that he was being held by a little girl.

"Monster?"

"Yeah . . . but now they call me something else."

He looked kind of embarrassed. "They call me Fluffy," he said.

I asked what had happened after I'd left him at the Control place.

"Well, I never made it out of there. They grabbed me before I could get a single cage opened. Not having opposable thumbs kind of slowed me down."

"I feel bad about that," I said. "I should have stayed to help."

"It was a dumb idea, anyway. And it turned out OK for both of us. I heard all about you being a hero and all."

"I'm no hero," I told him. "I was just trying to help my human."

"But didn't you try to jump the human with the gun?"

"No, not really. I was trying to get him to chase me, so my human and his friends could get away."

"Well, that's still pretty heroic in my book. You're a credit to our species."

"But what about you?" I asked. "Do you still bite people?"

"No, I gave that up. You know, I was wrong about that Control place. They didn't want to hurt us—they wanted to help. All that stuff was just a bunch of FLF propaganda. Lilly—that's my human's name—would have never found me if it hadn't been for them.

"I wouldn't bite her or any human—unless they tried to hurt her."

Chapter Twenty-Two. West 82nd Street.
I Write a Tell-All Book—this One.

Every Monday night, the Sarge and the Vet would go to their meeting. They never asked me to go, which was just as well. There's a lot of good TV on Monday nights.

It seemed that every other night that female reporter would come over. Sometimes she and the Sarge would go to a movie or something; other times she'd cook us dinner. She still talked too much, but she was OK.

Even weeks later, people were still interested in the Sarge and me. They even offered him a book deal, but he turned that down, too.

But I figured somebody should tell our story. And without opposable thumbs, typing would be kind of hard for me. The female reporter was going to help. But she decided people might think she was "exploiting" the Sarge and me.

So she found a human in California who had developed something called "an app" that translates Cat into human, and he agreed to let me try it out. Then she got a human who knows about commas and things to write down everything the computer translated.

I'm sure glad she found those humans.

Otherwise, I alone would have been left to tell the tale. And you probably wouldn't have understood a word of it.

About the Authors

Jon is an advertising copywriter and creative director who lives with his wife, Dianne, and a cat named Boo in Stamford, Connecticut. Jon figured that after thirty or so years of writing ads and commercials, he'd try writing something that doesn't try and sell anybody anything. Except maybe this book.

The Boo who inspired this book is a gentle soul who adopted Jon and Dianne Saunders as his humans after his own time on the streets. He's named for the Boo Radley character in Harper Lee's *To Kill a Mockingbird*. For like Mr. Radley, one of his favorite pastimes is watching the neighborhood children play, almost as if he were watching over them. When he's not so occupied, he enjoys eating, sleeping, and having his long, black hair brushed.

www.ingramcontent.com/pod-product-compliance
Lightning Source LLC
Chambersburg PA
CBHW050900180626
46814CB00007B/2820